FRATERNITY
OF
FRACTURES

FRATERNITY OF FRACTURES

MARK PANNEBECKER

authorHOUSE®

AuthorHouse™
1663 Liberty Drive
Bloomington, IN 47403
www.authorhouse.com
Phone: 1 (800) 839-8640

Author's photo by Steve Truesdell Photography
stevetruesdellphotography.com
Cover design by Mark Pannebecker and Steve Truesdell
Editing by Diana Blaylock

Published by AuthorHouse   03/23/2016

ISBN: 978-1-5049-5755-7 (sc)
ISBN: 978-1-5049-5754-0 (e)

Library of Congress Control Number: 2015917504

Print information available on the last page.

Any people depicted in stock imagery provided by Thinkstock are models,
and such images are being used for illustrative purposes only.
Certain stock imagery © Thinkstock.

This book is printed on acid-free paper.

CHAPTER 1

It was a perfect time for a robbery. Any earlier and there'd be too many people walking around; any later and the bars would be closing, causing too much activity; and later still, it would be unsafe as well as raise suspicion. Phoenix knew what she was doing.

She sat in her car listening to the Dead Kennedys, watching the thick smoke from the corner Vietnamese restaurant roll out from the exhaust fan and hang there ten feet above the sidewalk; she could smell the familiar spices of Asian cooking. The white smoke stagnating in the stale air added to her discomfort and she hoped for a breeze to cool her off.

Phoenix didn't want to sit under the dimly lit, haloed streetlights for too long and draw attention to herself, but she saw a squad car in the rearview mirror nestled in the oncoming traffic and decided to wait; but just sitting there made her feel heavy, the gray St. Louis sky weighed her down. She started to sweat and looked again in her rearview mirror. To keep her mind off the suffocating weather she thought about the security system of Chin's Orient Emporium and went through a mental list of what she needed to do to break it. The short rush of traffic finally drove past her, spiraling the cloud of smoke from the restaurant and sending it clutching into the night like skeleton fingers. The half-dozen cars continued down the two mile stretch of Grand Boulevard lined with inexpensive restaurants, cheap retail shops, and boarded-up buildings. When it was clear, Phoenix checked the area one more time: a handful of people, a couple of parked cars, little activity this time of night in the Tower Grove neighborhood.

She grabbed her Walkman and a cassette tape as she prepared to walk the block in a half to Chin's Orient Emporium. When she stepped out of her car, she was immediately wrapped in the humid July weather, her black one-piece, tight around her five-foot frame, stuck to her body as she moved her oversized black nylon bag onto her tenuous shoulders.

Standing outside the building, shrouded in its shadow, Phoenix slipped surgical gloves onto her fine hands. Partly protected by the blue haze of the new moon's light, she grabbed her small metal Mac flashlight, a pocket-sized version of what the police carry and a present from Justin Sunder, her friend and mentor, the first night they danced together. When she turned the head of her flashlight a strong white beam shot out and landed precisely on the store's telephone line. Phoenix stood in her suit of night, poised in the dark, her muscles tight, her jaw slightly clenched, and her nipples hard. Her large green eyes followed the narrow, focused light as she traced the phone line down the side of the two-story building. When she heard a couple approaching, she quickly turned off the light, pressed against the building, and squinted.

"Your eyes are like beacons in the night," Justin once told her, "close them." She wished he were with her now because—although she was good—she wasn't as good as Justin Sunder. Even though she knew Chin's system could be easily breached she still felt a little uncomfortable dancing alone for the first time since meeting him two years ago. She had come to depend on his expertise. And she enjoyed dancing with him.

Her eyelids dropped to form two crescent moons while waiting for the couple to pass. When it was safe, she opened her eyes again, turned the light back on, and continued to track the correct wire to the security box that flashed a red light. Phoenix knew with a system like this, bells and whistles went off if someone broke a window because the concern wasn't to catch the criminals but to draw attention to their activity. With a quick snip, she disabled the security system Chin's employed. In the distance a police siren sang, but Phoenix wasn't concerned—as Justin was prone to say, "It's the ones you don't hear that get you." Phoenix took black electrical tape and connected the severed lines so they appeared to be undamaged.

In the back, she found the small window she needed, just large and low enough for her to climb through. She covered the window with duct tape then tapped it several times with her flashlight, the muffled noise of breaking glass barely audible. She peeled away the gray tape, quietly bringing the broken glass with it, leaving a clean hole for her to enter through.

Once inside she felt comfortable again, the familiar feeling of excitement and confidence returned, and she took her time. Phoenix knew what she wanted. She didn't steal everything she could get her hands on, when she wanted a VCR she broke into a store and took a VCR, she didn't loot the place; she didn't break windows and grab whatever she could to sell later, that was for amateurs and punks; she didn't shoplift and she wasn't a kleptomaniac. She practiced her art with deliberation. Inside Chin's Orient Emporium, she only wanted three items. Her eyes quickly adjusted to the dark and she made her way through the store, straight for the kimono rack. She tried on several styles, checking the mirror to see how they looked, and finally chose an ivory colored lace kimono with a large, hand-sewn rose stitched on the back. She then walked over to the display case that housed the legal weapons. Using her lock-pick set, she opened the case for her second item. Phoenix slid open the glass panel and picked out a Balisong knife with red handles and a black tempered-steel blade, exactly like the butterfly knife she lost last year, the one her girlfriend Dena gave to her in New Orleans. She flicked her wrist three times and the six-inch blade shot out, revealing a deadly weapon in less than a second. She skillfully opened and closed it several times—like Dena had taught her.

"You're gonna hafta look out for yourself now, Phoenix," Dena said just before leaving New Orleans. "I'm not gonna be around to protect you from assholes that can't leave pretty thangs like you alone."

"Pretty thangs"—the phrase echoed in Phoenix's mind—she loved the way Dena said 'pretty thang' to her, like it was a precious title. She hadn't thought about her for years, and for a moment she and Dena were together again, saying good-bye. Phoenix touching Dena's flawless dark face, her cropped white hair, kissing her full lips one last time and pressing against her. Phoenix began to touch herself but then a light flashed on the side of the building and Phoenix was thrown back to St. Louis—Chin's. If the cop controlling the searchlight had better aim, he would have lit up Phoenix through the window, surprising her like a deer caught in headlights. She quickly dropped to the floor. When the officer positioned his light to shine through the window, Phoenix was already hidden. The cop slowly panned it across the store, illuminating the clothing racks; a full-length mirror that reflected the light onto the video shelf; onto the cash register above the weapons counter; and then across an opened curtain in the changing room against the back wall. Satisfied that nothing was wrong, the police slowly drove off, shining the light past the security box and then down along the row of storefronts.

After the store became dark again, Phoenix rolled out from under the counter and went over to the robes. She picked out the last item she wanted: a thick, hooded green robe, intricately and elaborately decorated with a dragon. Phoenix smiled as she pushed the heavy back door open and walked out into the alley, recalling the week before when she innocently walked into Chin's to simply browse but after recognizing the store's security system, and instantly knowing its faults, decided to dance there instead. She hit play on her Walkman and listened to Patti Smith as she ambled back to her car.

CHAPTER 2

Justin Sunder sat quietly on a barstool in John Bowman's bar and thought of Phoenix—he hadn't seen her all night and was worried; he wondered where she was, what she was doing. As he finished his drink, he casually looked in the mirror behind the bar. The image reflected back to him was that of his maternal grandfather who Justin had never met but saw once in an old photograph. Justin's mother, who did her best to remove any connection to her Native American ancestry, had shown him the old, faded black-and-white print taken when she was five and still living on the Northern Cheyenne Indian Reservation. She showed Justin the photograph to compare the squalor she lived in as a child to the comfort and wealth she now enjoyed in Kansas City. His grandfather, Standing Bear, had fought against Custer and continued to fight the U.S. government, up until his death, by refusing to become a citizen of the United States and advocating an independent Indian nation. The mirror reflected Justin's light brown skin and strong features. His dark brown eyes stopped for a moment on his scar—a third-degree burn on the side of his right cheek that continued down his neck to his collarbone, the seared skin shaped like Italy. His long, thick black hair, pulled back into a French braid, and the crew neck shirt he wore, revealed most of the scar that marred his otherwise handsome face.

He turned his gaze to John Bowman, the owner, who worked the bar like a consummate professional. On a busy night he'd go down the length of the bar, taking a dozen orders from a dozen different people, and return a minute later with the right drinks for the right person. John was a big, bearded man who moved with the agility of a dancer behind the narrow bar. He always wore a T-shirt with a cartoon character on it, and on this uncommonly slow night, he was wearing Captain America.

Patsy Cline came on as John, noticing Justin's empty glass, came over. "How ya' doin' there Justin?"

Justin smiled. "Another, when you get a chance."

John nodded and turned his attention to a young woman who came up to the bar. She smiled at Justin, but when she saw the third-degree burn on his face, she quickly turned to John and ordered two Zinfandels. Her rude behavior toward Justin did not go unnoticed by John who made Justin's drink and took his time before splashing the cheap wine into two glasses.

John didn't know why, but his bar got people from all over St. Louis. This lady with her wine fit immediately into the look he facetiously referred to as 'west county', whether they were actually from the suburbs or not; the boys in the back playing pool were clearly from the south side; and the party sitting at the tables opposite the bar were probably from the city's west end because of their flamboyant behavior. The eclectic mix gave J.B.'s a certain attitude, and recently his bar had become a popular hangout. He didn't know they were there because of his unique taste. John adorned his bar with whatever he liked with no regard to what people thought. The result was a strange collection of miscellaneous items that eventually drew his current staff to apply. The staff, as well as the customers, gave him too much credit for his creativity; it wasn't a conscious effort he put into decorating his bar—he just did what he liked. The same was with his choice in music.

"Three Cigarettes (In An Ashtray)" played from the four speakers hanging at each corner. John, while wiping down the bar, looked up and saw the younger brother of an old friend approaching with a familiar stride.

Dylan Panicosky had just recently started coming to J.B.'s. His physique, his confidence, and his soft, almost feminine features— Dylan, like his brother Billy, could only grow wisps of facial hair and both brothers opted for a clean, shaven look—reminded John of Billy Panicosky, whom John used to ride with occasionally before Billy was killed. Billy the Kid, as his friends and his motorcycle club called him, was the road captain for the Four Horseman.

"My lover and I, in a small cafe..." Dylan sang along, "Then a stranger came along, and everything went wrong—hey Johnny I accidentally broke this glass, the damn thing just fell over. It wasn't my fault, I wasn't even there." Dylan smiled and handed John the remains, "Sorry, man, can I get two more Buds from ya?" While waiting for his beers, Dylan continued to keep the beat with his hands, softly tapping on the sheet metal bar. He looked over at Justin, and they both nodded to each other. Then Dylan did something few men have ever done to Justin Sunder. Noticing Justin's scar, Dylan paused for a respectful moment on the wound, acknowledging it, and when he locked eyes with Justin's, he simply nodded. Justin nodded back, and Dylan, knocking on the bar once as if the matter was settled, turned to John Bowman for his beers.

Phoenix left the Tower Grove neighborhood and drove east down Highway 44 where late-night construction was underway; causing the drive home to the apartment she shared with Justin to take almost 40 minutes. She pulled onto the dimly lit Lafayette Avenue and drove past the black, empty, broken eyes of the deserted city hospital to the old French neighborhood of Soulard where she'd lived since she first rolled into St. Louis last year.

When she pulled around the corner, she saw lights on in the living room of their apartment. She thought Justin was home and smiled. Their building, analogous of French Renaissance, had been renovated into loft-style apartments and theirs was a 2,500 square foot rectangle warehouse on the third floor. When the annual Soulard Mardi Gras parade would crawl past they would stand out on their wrought iron balcony and playfully show their breasts.

She parked in the back alley and walked up the iron steps. When she reached the back porch the security light came on, flooding her from above. She unlocked the back door and entered. The only new walls constructed were along the north side where Phoenix's bedroom, facing east into the alley, and Justin's bedroom, facing west onto the street, were separated by a large kitchen. Each bedroom had a private bathroom. As soon as Phoenix walked in, she could see her friend wasn't home. The track lighting, on the south, unpainted brick wall, lit up nine original posters advertising obscure foreign plays and products from the 1920s, several limited addition prints of photographs from national and international artists, and many original paintings and works of art from the postmodernist movement. Phoenix crossed the wooden floors to the open living room, threw her bag on the leather Eileen Gray sofa, and sat down.

The living room, defined by two large area rugs from France, was furnished partly in stolen goods—a testament to her and Justin's craft—and furniture Justin bought in the mid-eighties right after he moved to St. Louis. The expensive European imported furniture complemented the open, airy feeling of the loft. The dramatic designs of bent steel and leather from Le Corbusier; the Italian marble and thick glass; the black lacquered wood and tightly woven fabric gave the apartment a clean, stylish look. Justin taught Phoenix about designers like Isamu Noguchi, Charles Mackintosh, and Ludwig Mies Van Der Rohe. He had walked with her in an exclusive store downtown telling her about the Bauhaus movement and pointing out the history of some of their designs and what made them unique. He also helped her pick out some of the better pieces by contemporary designers like Philippe Starck and Peter Maly, and Phoenix soon understood what gave one thing style and made another a cheap imitation or gaudy.

Phoenix scanned the shelves of cassettes and albums that filled an area between two industrial style, floor-length windows. The alphabetized collection sorted by genre, was an impressive look into the history of music, from classical to new wave. Phoenix, unable to decide what she wanted to hear, decided to just play whatever Justin had been listening to. When Roxy Music's *Slave to Love* came on, she smiled and turned up the volume and surrounded herself with the sultry music. Reaching into her bag, she pulled out the green robe she picked out for

Justin and inspected it one more time as she walked into his bedroom. She folded it neatly and placed it on his bed.

Justin's austere bedroom contrasted with the elegance of the rest of their apartment. The old wooden dresser in the corner was one Phoenix found in an alley in the summer of '86 just before she met him. After they moved in together, he offered his German-made dresser to Phoenix and took hers. On the wooden floor laid a cheap rug Phoenix bought for $20. And Justin's bed was a simple futon covered with Egyptian cotton sheets. If it wasn't for the hidden gun collection housed inside the armoire, Justin's room could have been a monk's quarters.

Walking back into the living room, she saw the flashing red light of the answering machine sitting next to a new beige Macintosh 512K computer that neither one ever used. She went over to the small marble-topped desk and hit play: "Hi," Justin's voice came on, "It's me, I'm down at J.B.'s with Bernard if you want to join us. Bye."

CHAPTER 3

Phoenix walked through the door of J.B.'s, nodding at the bouncer as she passed, and called out to John. Both Justin and Dylan—who was ordering another round—looked over and watched her walk in, wearing the same tight fitting, black cat suit she wore earlier.

John smiled. "Evening, ma'am."

Phoenix approached the bar, looking closer at John's shirt. "Who's *that*?"

"Captain America. What the hell's wrong with you?"

"Of course." She smiled at John. "Captain America," She said as she pulled up a barstool next to Justin, "I liked the Thor one better."

Phoenix gave Justin a kiss on the cheek and Justin took a moment to take in her natural scent of Jasmine. She looked over and saw Dylan pay for his beers with crumbled up ones and change. When he saw her looking his way, he smiled and winked. Phoenix politely smiled back, turned back to Justin, and grabbed his drink.

"So, where've you been hiding?" He asked.

"Nowhere, just shopping."

"Really?"

"Yeah, and I got something for you, too."

"Aw, ya shouldn't have. What I get?"

"You'll see later—Hey, John, can I get a Tanqueray and tonic?"

Justin looked again at Phoenix's cat suit. "Wait a minute, shopping? Where?"

"Chin's," she said into Justin's drink.

"You danced there anyway?" Justin asked, masking his concern behind irritation.

"You said you didn't wanna dance there."

"Yeah, but I didn't think you'd go—" Justin stopped himself as John brought over her drink then walked away. "Without me," he finished.

"Justin," Phoenix began adamantly, "if you don't wanna do small businesses anymore, that's fine, I accept that but *I'm* gonna keep doing what I wanna do. Don't try to manipulate me. It ain't gonna work, baby." She smiled and pulled out a cigarette.

Justin immediately pulled out his silver Zippo and lit her cigarette. "You shouldn't have done it alone, that's all I'm saying," he offered as a way of apology then finished the last sip of his drink left by Phoenix. "I'm glad you made it," he said, reaching over for Phoenix's drink.

"So am I!" Bernard interrupted from behind. "Justin went into another one of his somber, narcoleptic-inducing moods and was getting absolutely boring!" he said, hugging Phoenix with his sinewy arms. On his forearm closest to Justin, Bernard had a tattoo of colorful feathers surrounding a black ankh. He added the feathers after meeting Justin and learning he was Cheyenne.

"Not as boring as you being on the phone for 40 minutes," Justin returned.

"What can I say, I'm addicted to those 900 numbers." Bernard winked at Phoenix.

"I'm happy to hear you practice safe sex," she said.

"And honey, it's the only way I can get it lately! Let me tell you, I should put on a habit and join a nunnery. I'm already halfway there!" Bernard let out a short, high-pitched scream directed more to the boys sitting at the table behind them than anyone else.

When Dylan Panicosky approached the bar again, Bernard was the first to see him and he let out a little grunt and a nudge to Phoenix, who turned to see whom the grunt was for. A little game they played. When she saw the pretty stranger again, she responded with a little grunt of her own. Dylan walked, deliberately, toward her. His intensity cut through the grunting Bernard and Phoenix playfully continued, and Phoenix stopped. Justin, like a sparrow sensing a hawk, watched Dylan sidle up to Phoenix and grab a handful of pretzels.

"Hi," Dylan said to Phoenix, soberly and without a smile. His eyes fixed on hers.

Phoenix, captivated by Dylan's presence just stared at him. Defiantly but without malice, as if to say: Yeah, now what? Phoenix had found few men whose next move worked on her.

Dylan glanced over to Justin, and then to Bernard. Dylan prided himself on his powers of observation, and he thought he had this one figured out. He took a half step toward Phoenix and smiled softly, his dark eyes reflecting in her green. He held it there for a just a moment, and then gracefully walked toward the door.

"Who's that boy?" Bernard asked after Dylan left.

"Don't know." Phoenix watched him in the large mirror behind the bar walk past the windows.

After a moment Justin spoke up: "Oh, please, will you two dry your panties?"

Phoenix picked up a handful of pretzels and tossed them at Justin, who returned in kind with his own pretzel bombardment. Bernard soon followed and John, seeing the pretzels flying, yelled to them: "Knock it off down there!" Slowly they stopped.

Bernard finally sealed the excitement by declaring he needed to leave and asked Justin to give him a ride home.

"I just got my drink," Phoenix pointed out.

"I know," Bernard said in mock sarcasm, "and I'm truly sorry, but I have to meet up with a friend of mine. So, you can keep your tight little no-panty-line-wearing tight ass here or you can come with—and if you do come, I don't want to smell it—fish."

"Fag."

"Well, at least I can decide which sex I want!"

Phoenix laughed and reached down to grab Bernard between the legs who adroitly blocked her attempt to maim him. Bernard jumped onto Justin's lap and gave him a kiss on his cheek. "Save me from this wicked woman!"

"Save yourself. And get off my lap, you weigh a ton!"

"I certainly do not!"

Justin picked up Bernard. "Come on, let's go bye-bye," he said, walking out the door with Bernard in his arms who then waved at the boys sitting at the table behind them.

Phoenix finished her drink in one swallow. "Okay, let's go."

"Yeah, and quickly, before someone drops a house on her."

CHAPTER 4

The three traveled west on Highway 40 in Justin's white Nova, listening to Depeche Mode sing about strange love. Phoenix, sitting between Justin and Bernard, lit a joint and passed it to Bernard while Justin maneuvered around a semi transporting a mobile home. Justin put in Peter Gabriel

"When are you going to fix these shocks? I feel like I'm riding a horse here." Bernard handed Justin the joint.

"Don't ride a horse, Bernard," Justin said, "bestiality doesn't suit you."

"My celibacy doesn't extend to the animal kingdom."

"Yuck," Phoenix added, taking the joint from Justin.

"I saw a video once with a woman and a donkey. It's the most bizarre thing you've ever seen."

"Yuck again."

"I knew a woman that let her dog lick her," Bernard offered the conversation.

"Lesbians are big on that."

"They are not."

"No, it's quite the popular act for women, sexually deviate as it may be," Justin joked.

"You two guys are the deviates."

"Hey, I've never shaved a hamster," Bernard said.

"No, he likes the way the fur feels on the walls of his ass," Justin added.

They approached an intricate neon advertisement for Anheuser-Busch. The large, multi-colored neon eagle moved its wings, giving the illusion of flight.

"That would be a true test of our skills, Phoenix," Justin said, "the Busch mansion."

"Where is it?"

"Grant's Farm."

"*Grant's* Farm? Shouldn't it be Busch's Farm?" Phoenix asked.

"It was Ulysses S. Grant's farm before August Busch bought it and built his mansion there."

"Yeah, it's suppose to have a moat," Bernard said.

"A moat, huh?" Phoenix paused, thinking. "That would be a challenge."

"Honey, you're not that good."

"Not yet, anyway," Justin said.

"You guys are just afraid to set goals."

"What do you mean, *you* guys? Don't drag me into your sordid little lives. I'm an honest man," said Bernard, finishing the joint.

Justin and Phoenix let out a simultaneous exclamation, which Bernard countered with insistence that he was telling the truth.

Justin got off at Grand and drove down the vacant boulevard.

"Why'd we go up 40?" Bernard asked, inferring Highway 44 would have been quicker.

"They're beginning late-night construction on 44, and I didn't want to get caught in the exodus from all the drunks leaving the Landing."

"They weren't there earlier," Phoenix said.

"They started at midnight."

"How do you know these things?" Bernard asked, impressed.

"It's my job to know these things," Justin said. "Besides, they had signs up."

"Oh, so it's a reading thing?"

After they past the old Compton Hill water tower—a 179-foot tall phallic structure of brick and stone with French Romanesque features—they saw the flashing lights of police cars strobing the area around Chin's.

An hour after Phoenix had left Chin's, the owner came in accompanied by a fat, blond prostitute he picked up on the south-side stroll. During his sadistic sex with his masochistic partner, he looked over at the weapons case and saw it had been jimmied open. After reaching his climax, he sent the girl away, cleaned up, then called the police from the pay phone across the street.

Phoenix and Justin smiled at each other as they passed Chin's and continued to Bernard's apartment. On a side street, they had to slow down to give several people standing in the middle of the street a chance to move out of the way. Shadowed faces stared at them as they drove by. A row of streetlights was out between a condemned building and an old apartment complex, momentarily pitching the Nova into darkness. When they passed an abandoned house, Phoenix thought she saw someone moving inside. Justin pulled down Bernard's well-lit cul-de-sac and parked in front of a large Victorian-style townhouse. They said their good-byes and Bernard walked into his house.

Justin remained parked, looking at the building and admiring the architecture, lost for a moment in the tiled mansard roof, dormer windows, and the intricate cornice. Justin tried to make out the sculpture in low relief ornamenting the horizontal frieze below the cornice but couldn't.

The Tower Grove neighborhood, once considered by a select elite an ideal place to build 'country' homes, became a popular neighborhood for the rich when St. Louis started to grow. Most of the remaining buildings of that era retained the detail of excellence evident in Bernard's converted townhouse. Other houses had battlement parapets and decorative brackets under low-pitched roofs. Across the street, an apartment was designed in the Italianate style, the corner brickwork accentuated by rustic quoins.

"What's up?" Phoenix interrupted Justin's thoughts.

"I was just looking at these buildings."

"No, let's go home," she said, misinterpreting his comment and thinking he wanted to dance.

"There's some really nice architecture in St. Louis," Justin said to the building and its long-dead architect.

"Yeah, and that's about it."

Justin smiled. "And cheap rent."

"Yeah, and cheap rent, that too." Phoenix turned her head and looked out the window at an ivy-covered apartment building across the street. The night had cooled off and the night was as quiet as an abandoned town.

Justin was about to pull away when Phoenix whispered his name, "Justin, look." She pointed to a young man, who looked familiar to her, sneaking around the side of the building.

"What's he carrying, a crowbar?"

"Looks like it."

They watched him disappear around the corner.

"You want to stick around and watch this?" Justin asked, knowing the stranger was going to attempt a break-in.

"Sure, it'll be just like TV," Phoenix said just before the loud sounds of wood being forced away from its mooring was heard.

"In surround sound," Justin added.

"Amateur."

They heard more noise a moment later, this time coming from inside the apartment.

"A little loud, you think?"

"What's he doing in there... dancing?" Justin asked, and they both laughed at the private joke.

"This guy's an idiot. Let's go."

"No, let's see how it ends."

"Maybe when the cops come we'll get a car chase," Phoenix said, turning to the window. Caught in the moonlight, Phoenix looked ethereal, and Justin stared at her like he did every time she wasn't looking—a loving, soft, distant offering he saved only for the times she couldn't see the longing hiding behind his dark brown eyes.

It took all of Justin Sunder's strength to convince Phoenix he only wanted her friendship. He didn't want to jeopardize their relationship by telling her he still loved her. He feared Phoenix would leave him if she knew how he really felt; and he would rather be a friend in her company than an unrequited lover, alone, without her. It hurt him every time he looked into her sparkling green eyes with tender flecks of white and gold. He saw her soul behind those eyes. And the beauty there saddened him because he knew he could never touch that part of her as a lover.

"You want to move out of this sleeping town?" Justin asked.

"To where?"

"I don't know, New Mexico, Colorado, maybe Arizona."

"Sure, honey, whatever you want."

The noise from the apartment stopped and a moment later the pretty stranger from J.B.'s came around the corner carrying a suitcase.

"Hey, Justin, does he look familiar?"

Justin looked closer and remembered him from the bar. "I'll be damned, this is a small town."

CHAPTER 5

"I bought it," John Bowman said to Phoenix, referring to the bike parts montage hanging on the wall of his bar, "from my cousin—jeez—about 20 years ago, half-buried in mud in his backyard. Tommy rode her maybe 100 miles after he bought her and dumped her down in Hermann, Missouri. It was an accident anybody could'a had—although the wine he drank down there probably didn't help." He laughed and Phoenix smiled. "Anyway, he broke his arm and hip and decided he'd come as close to a mangled death as he wanted to get. Tommy was never the kind of guy to push his luck, ya know? He didn't want to ride that horse no more. He almost left her down there but my uncle convinced him to bring her home. When he did, he just dumped her in his backyard—I mean really dumped her—he rolled her into his back yard and just let her drop. About a year later, I bought her. I only had to rebuild the carbs to get her running again.

"So how did it end up on your wall?

"She'd been abused too much and just couldn't run anymore. There was a lot of internal damage, no compression, this and that. I would've had to eventually rebuild the whole engine; and I didn't feel like doing it at the time. So, I used her good parts for my next bike; kinda like if I had this girl's body and that girl's face and this girl's personality, you know, and mixed them all together, I'd have the perfect woman. It was the same with my bike."

"Why do you bikers always talk about your bikes as if they're women?"

"Out of respect, you know? It's like a ship, but it's more than that. There's a bond there, like the bond you make with a woman."

Phoenix knew what he meant; she'd seen it before. When she lived in Florida, she knew a biker there, Wood, who washed his bike more than he bathed himself. His bike shined from the chrome surrounding the red metal frame. The spokes sparkled as they caught the sun's rays or a streetlamp's glow. Wood's bike had no imperfections, unlike Wood, whose body and soul were as ripped, marred and torn as the leathers he wore. His emblem, a bonsai tree, was embossed on his gas tank.

"I prune myself and the people around me like the bonsai," he remarked with callousness. Wood's self-preservation could be frightening. But Phoenix knew with the bonsai the pruning, the sacrifice, was needed. In the end, what remained was beautiful, strong, and unique.

"Then why'd you abandon her once you realized it was going to take a little work to keep things running?" she asked John.

"Ah, Phoenix, if I knew then what I know now, I would'a kept her; but when you're young you do stupid things."

"So what about your Indian now? Did you adjust the timing yet?"

"No, I've been too busy."

"You can't find time to fix your motorcycle? What kinda biker are you?"

"I'll get to it when I get to it, ya know? When the time is right. Everything when the time is right."

"Well, do it for God's sake. I wanna ride."

John laughed, "Yes ma'am."

When Dylan Panicosky walked in he immediately recognized Phoenix and made a beeline to John. After ordering a beer, Dylan squared his shoulders and looked into the mirror at Phoenix's reflection.

"Where's your suitcase?" She asked his likeness in the mirror.

Dylan laughed, "What? Are we going somewhere?"

"Never know."

John stepped between their dialogue in the mirror. "You two know each other?"

Phoenix offered her hand to Dylan who gently accepted it. When they touched a slight surge of energy, like an opium rush, simultaneously shot through them. They both felt it and their response was the same: their peripheral vision became almost nonexistent, turning their image of each other into a displaced apparition that floated in a tunnel, moving closer to each other. The noises in the bar got lost in the heartbeat heard in their ears. Dylan smelled Jasmine; Phoenix, rust. Neither had felt skin so soft, as if they were at risk of sharing atoms. It was a lingering, shared hallucination that lasted only moments in real time but both felt they had been drifting there forever.

Dylan was the first to let go and Phoenix, no longer tethered to Dylan, wiped her sweaty palms on her thighs and became aroused by her own touch. She wondered if Dylan had touched her again. The two realized they'd shared a rare experience. Any awkwardness in their first meeting was instantly removed in that intimate moment.

But then suddenly Dylan turned to John and asked him, "So, what were you two talking about?"

John told Dylan the story of how his Triumph ended up on J.B.'s wall. During the story, Dylan moved closer to Phoenix and rested his foot on her bar stool's foot rung, lightly touching her leg. Dylan listened, offering insightful comments and observations, and saw Phoenix out of the corner of his eye, watching him. He threw in humorous anecdotes to accompany the tale and listened to Phoenix laugh. When John was called away, Dylan turned to Phoenix and moved closer so they were almost touching, and waited for her to say something.

Phoenix waited in anticipation for Dylan's leg, his arm, any part of his body, to touch her. She moved in her seat and brushed against him. Dylan, never taking his eyes away from Phoenix's, lit a cigarette. Phoenix shifted in her seat and adjusted her posture. She had never met a man who stared into her eyes like Dylan did; she was never more aware of her own eyes than at that moment.

"I saw you last week," Phoenix finally said after she broke the connection reaching for her drink.

"And I saw you," Dylan said and smiled, still holding her eyes when she turned back to look at him.

Phoenix took a drink. "I saw you break into someone's apartment."

Dylan looked down at the ashtray and flicked his cigarette. Phoenix, pleased at this brief interruption from Dylan's piercing fascination, relaxed.

"You saw that, huh?" He looked up and asked with a grin.

Phoenix nodded and smiled.

"I didn't really, technically, break in. My ex-girlfriend finally had the good sense to throw me out, and I was just collecting a few things."

"Why'd she throw you out?"

"I wouldn't marry her." He took a sip of Phoenix's drink.

"Some people still believe in fairy tales," she said, taking her drink back and setting it down in front of her.

Dylan put out his cigarette and looked around the bar. "Do you want to play a game?" he asked, motioning to the pool table.

"I think you're playing one now."

Dylan smiled, "Pool. An innocent game of pool, that's all."

"Yeah, sure."

John, at the end of the bar, watched them walk past, and thought of Justin.

CHAPTER 6

While Phoenix and Dylan became acquainted, Justin had dinner with Sharon, a tall, gangly brunette with a slight overbite, whom he first met three years ago when he attended the Architecture School of Washington University. Their friendship started fading after Justin dropped out of school and started dancing with Phoenix. The reasons he gave for leaving, to Sharon and a few others, were questionable and most thought he just couldn't afford it anymore.

He ran into her while buying fruit and vegetables at the Soulard Farmers' Market, and they decided to get together for dinner that night. While eating at one of the better steakhouses in St. Louis, they talked about the school, its professors, the remaining students they knew, and Sharon's plans after graduation.

"You should go back," Sharon said after dinner. "If you can."

"If I do it won't be for architecture or design."

"Why not? You designed some great stuff."

Justin thought about telling her that those great designs were made by his younger brother, Matthew, but decided against it. Matthew, who displayed a natural talent at an early age, used to build skyscrapers with his Popsicle sticks. Even with his Lincoln Logs, he showed an understanding of form and function and design. Their father, Nathan Sunder, was especially proud of his youngest son's ability and praised him constantly. Matthew inherited Nathan's interest in architecture as well as Nathan's flatfeet, fair hair, fair skin and round body. All of Justin's attempts to win his father's affection in architecture and design failed. Matthew was the genius of the family. If he hadn't been murdered at 18 his talents would have undoubtedly surpassed his father's. After Matthew's death, Justin picked up the gauntlet—not so much for his father, but for his brother. At Wash U., Justin respectfully offered the dozen designs made by Matthew Sunder. Eventually Justin came to the sobering realization that he didn't belong there; he had the interest and the desire but not the talent nor the passion of his brother, and soon even the desire left him.

The conversation with Sharon brought back many unpleasant memories for Justin. Sharon didn't have the talent either, and her desire was rooted only in the monetary rewards of simple high-rises and ranch-style homes. She reminded him of his father who designed simple or gaudy structures, depending on the nouveau riche client at the time. *She should go work for him*, Justin thought. He remembered Sharon didn't even know the Soulard Market's design was Italian Renaissance—he had to tell her it was, specifically, reminiscent of Brunelleschi's hospital in Florence. He wanted the night to end.

"I even thought about being a movie producer at on point," Sharon started, "because they make lots of money, but I was always good at drawing buildings and designing stuff so I decided to do this. I mean I couldn't have pursued a liberal arts degree—could you imagine me a starving artist?" She paused for a moment, then offered a joke, "Besides, I hate blood, so I couldn't be a doctor. What were my choices?"

"You could've become a lawyer."

Sharon laughed, "Are you kidding? That market is totally saturated!"

"What about accounting?"

"Nah, I can't interface with numbers." There was a long pause in the dinner conversation. The crème brulee couldn't come fast enough for Justin.

"So," Sharon offered, "what do you think about Reagan winning his second term? That's pretty good, huh?"

———————————————

At J.B.'s, Dylan and Phoenix played pool against two guys who'd held the table for the last two hours. Dylan took a shot that missed its intended target and bounced around, hitting three bumpers without coming in contact with anything, until it hit the eight ball and tapped it into the corner pocket.

"Nice shot. You're quite a shark."

"I wanted to quit anyway."

"Mission accomplished then, well done."

David, a tall man wearing clean, starched and pressed clothes rose from a church pew against the wall and walked straight over to Phoenix and rudely grabbed the cue stick away from her. Phoenix glared at him and was about to grab the cue back, but in a rare submissive response, decided to walk away instead. She had been on her own long enough to know when to avoid certain situations. Dylan, on the other hand, didn't care about avoiding situations. He immediately grabbed the stick out of David's hands and took one step closer to him.

Kevin, a big man with black-framed glasses and a thick goatee, came up and stood by his friend David. The two towers of men stood shoulder to shoulder, facing Dylan.

"Don't ever do that again," Dylan Panicosky said to David, slowly, enunciating every word clearly, his teeth clenched. "You fuck with her and you fuck with me, and you don't wanna fuck with me." He stared at David and waited for a response.

David glanced over at John Bowman, then over to the bouncer, then at Dylan, and assessing no real threat by any of them, finally turned to Kevin and offered a little grin. But Dylan's strong silence and his clear intent earned David's respect.

"May I have the stick?" David asked still grinning, looking down at Dylan who was a foot shorter.

Dylan tossed the cue onto the table and joined Phoenix at the bar.

After Dylan left, David said to Kevin, "'Fuck with her and you fuck with me.' Yeah, maybe I'll just fuck you both." He smiled and Kevin laughed. "Maybe after a few more drinks."

Phoenix had two beers waiting for Dylan. He took her hand and allowed her to lead him away to a booth near the door.

Dylan gazed at her soft brown hair, her large green eyes, her light brown skin, her lips that were slightly turned up at the corners, offering a perpetual smile...

"Where the hell did you come from?"

She laughed, "I was about to ask you the same question."

"Tell me something, Phoenix."

"What?"

"Anything."

Phoenix, trying to sum up her life and define herself, trying to think of how she could explain who she is, had no idea how to respond. She thought of offering something safe and silly (*I like peaches*), something trivial and non-bonding (*I'm a Scorpio*), but Dylan's eyes kept piercing through her concerns, worries, and fears. She had never met a man with such presence. His *presence* and the sense of trust it inspired made Phoenix think of Justin for a moment and the faith she had in Justin was transferred to Dylan. She knew she could tell Dylan anything and it would be accepted without judgment. She felt herself getting aroused at the possibilities with this beautiful man.

"I'm a thief."

"Yes you are."

"No, really. Well, more of a cat burglar. We—when, when I want a kimono, I'll break into a store and take a kimono. Someday I hope to up my game and be like David Niven in *The Pink Panther*."

"Wow."

"Yep. Your turn."

Dylan leaned over and kissed her for the first time. The kiss, soft and gentle, blended their beautiful features together in perfect symmetry like the folding of wings.

When they separated, Dylan excused himself. In the bathroom, he let out a sigh and used this time to remind himself that he needed to be cool. The women he showed his affections to too soon always backed away, but the women he showed indifference to—in the beginning -- always came back. Dylan's pattern had worked for him in the past, and he saw no reason to change it now. He returned to Phoenix and sat across from her in the booth.

"So," Dylan grabbed his beer bottle. "Why did you tell me you're a thief, I mean cat burglar, you don't even know me?" Dylan moved his arm to rest on the back of the booth and drank from his beer.

Phoenix observed Dylan. His eyes were now darting here and there as people walked in or passed by; and when he did look at her they lacked the power of before, but not the passion. She observed his body language as he sat across from her, sipping his beer, lighting his cigarette and flicking it at the ashtray. His intensity had shifted but it hadn't completely left his presence. She wondered if her blurting out that she was a thief was premature and a little irresponsible. She wondered if her obvious attraction to him intimidated him. When he lit another cigarette even though he already had one burning in the ashtray, Phoenix smiled.

"I guess I told you that to turn you on." She paused. "Or off." She shifted her position in the booth to mirror Dylan's and stared at him.

Dylan smiled, "I'm turned on by you, not your hobby," he said, putting out one of the cigarettes.

"It's more of a profession."

"Is there a tech school for that sort of thing?"

"Yeah, I'll introduce you to him."

"I'd like to join you sometime, if you don't mind. Or, we could go to a movie."

"You serious?" The thought of breaking into an apartment with this exquisite man turned her on. She crossed her legs under the table.

"I'm a very serious person."

"I'll let you know." She fantasized about Dylan and her in a dark apartment where they didn't belong. She could feel herself getting warm and squeezed her legs together, and thought about masturbating.

"Wait a minute, are we talking about a movie?" Phoenix asked, feeling herself flush.

"Hell no." Dylan got up, slid into Phoenix's side of the booth, and straddled her, his lower body pressed hard against hers. Phoenix pulled him to her and outlined his lips with her tongue. She grabbed the back of his hair and pulled him away.

"You're a dangerous man, Dylan Panicosky." Phoenix smiled.

"I'm not," he said, staring at his reflection in her green eyes.

CHAPTER 7

In his apartment, Justin stripped off his clothes and put on the green robe Phoenix stole for him. He watered the many plants throughout the house; at the indoor garden, he watered the aloe veras, ferns, yucca plants, and the assorted flowers. He poured the remaining water from the pitcher into a blue glass vase that held a single lily. He then walked over to his favorite chair, a leather and steel chaise lounge designed by Corbusier, and started reading. When Phoenix entered, he set the book aside. "Hi, honey."

She walked to Justin and handed him a pretzel. "Here, I brought you something."

Justin looked at the pretzel from J.B.'s and smiled. Phoenix sat on the floor next to him. "How was your date?"

"Not very good."

"I'm sorry."

"Don't be, I'm not. She belongs to a world alien to me. How was your night?"

"Well, I met an interesting boy," she said, smiling and went over to an end table by the sofa.

"Another one?"

Phoenix grabbed a bag of weed out of a drawer and started rolling a joint. "Remember the guy we saw breaking into that apartment over by Bernard's?"

"Him?"

"We might dance together sometime," she said, sitting down on the sofa across from Justin.

"What does that mean?" Justin rose up out of his chair. "What the fuck, Phoenix. Just because I don't want to do small businesses anymore, you're gonna bring in some kid you don't even know?" He sat next to Phoenix and lit her joint. "Now who's manipulating who?"

"Oh, please, will you stop? What do you think I'm gonna do, run off with this guy? I'd be lost without you; you know that. It's just a date. Here." She handed him the joint and Justin took a long hit.

"Yeah?" he said while holding his breath. "Then go to a movie if it's just a date." Justin exhaled, blowing smoke up toward the ceiling fan.

"Are you jealous? That's so cute! Now, knock it off."

"I was looking at a house in the West End the other night, you interested?" Justin asked.

"If that's the only way we'll dance together, sure."

"Phoenix, breaking into somebody's house is a lot less dangerous then these businesses you want to keep doing. Remember when we stole those?" He pointed to the foreign posters framed and hanging on the wall. They came across the vintage advertisements while out browsing one day and decided to come back for them later. But Justin misread the alarm system as movement detectors. When they got in and started smoking the place with a fine mist so they could see the sensor's light beams, he realized it was a temperature-sensitive system with a silent alarm, and the two quickly fled. To confuse the cops, Justin tossed a brick through a window. Two blocks away a squad car, without flashing lights or sirens, rushed passed them. A month later, they went back, properly prepared to counteract the system, and took the posters they wanted. Phoenix's favorite was an Absinth advertisement from Spain with a lone green devil uncorking a bottle; Justin's was an ad for a Parisian performance of Cyrano de Bergerac.

Phoenix looked again at the framed posters on the wall. "We came really close that time," Phoenix said, laughing.

"Too close."

"Oh, come on, Justin! These houses you want to do are boring. What do they have, simple alarms or no alarm at all? Where's the challenge in that? Why did you teach me all that stuff, if you don't expect me to use it?"

"I didn't want you to get caught."

"I'm not taking the easy road, Justin. There's an art to this and you know it, and until I get bored or busted I'm gonna keep pushing it. I don't do this for the same reasons you do."

"I know why you do it," Justin interrupted and smiled, knowing Phoenix's almost erotic response to dancing where she didn't belong.

"I never should have told you that!" Phoenix quickly grabbed the joint from Justin in mock anger, accidentally dropping it on his lap. Both jumped up and scrambled for the burning joint before it burnt a hole in the leather.

Justin laughed, "I'm just curious to find out what other fetishes you have."

Phoenix smiled back and continued their conversation. "Anyway, like I was saying—jerk—you have some sort of twisted Robin Hood logic, but I do it for the excitement. If it's not exciting, why do it?"

"You need a reason," Justin said, settling down again.

"I gave you my reason."

"It's got to be more than simple hedonism."

"No, it doesn't. That's exactly what it should be. That's why we're on this planet, to have a good time and nothing else matters. Not architecture, governments, those posters, children—none of that shit. Nothing matters in this world but to have a good time while you're here. If you're not happy now, when do you expect to be?"

"There's more to life than that. There's principles, ideals, morals..."

"Morals! Whose morals? And what the hell is that anyway?"

"I'm not talking about the morals the hypocrites in religion preach—love your neighbor but only if he follows your religion. I'm not using the definition of morality that capitalists use—the 'what's right for General Motors is right for America' bullshit. I'm talking about a different set of rules that governs people regardless of laws or customs or what we've been taught. Our morals may be different but they're just as valid. Just because we're thieves doesn't mean we're immoral. Breaking the law—for the right reason—is completely justifiable. Especially when it's a non-violent crime, like stealing—and stealing from the *wealthy* even more so. I have no problem with taking their toys, no problem at all, because the extreme wealthy are immoral. It's axiomatic. They eat their own. They literally kill their families, their business associates, their friends—for what? For what?"

"Money and power," Phoenix answered.

"Exactly. Successful, wealthy businessmen design unsafe cars, knowing they'll kill people; they sell their guns, wrapping themselves in the flag; they market deadly products with no regard for human life, only profit. They have no sense of *right*, only what's *legal*. But, I don't like taking from the small businessman. I've decided to draw the line there. I'll give them the benefit of the doubt."

"Small businessman, big businessman, it doesn't matter," Phoenix said. "They'd still pay their employees a dollar an hour if they could. They'd still hire children; they'd still demand a 60-hour workweek; they'd still have company stores. You give them too much credit, Justin."

"I'm an optimistic sort of guy"

"Bordering on delusional."

They both smiled at each other. Phoenix approached Justin and motioned him to slide off the couch and sit on the floor, which he did. Phoenix sat on the sofa with Justin between her legs and began to brush his long, dark hair.

"Delusional," he said. "Okay, I'll buy that."

"And one more thing: how do you know this guy in the West End isn't one of your small businessmen?"

"He's not, trust me. Besides, even if he is, the only thing I really want in there is his Uzi."

CHAPTER 8

Dark storm clouds formed early in the evening, hiding the stars and their constellations. The warm weather had taken an unexpected turn and the smell of rain waited in the cool night. After the wind ceased, the evening became calm and quiet. The only illumination came from the unbroken streetlights and the waxing moon.

Dylan Panicosky and Phoenix stood outside an apartment building in the bustling University City's *Loop*. Dylan smoked a cigarette while Phoenix leaned against the wall with her arms crossed. The two, in plain sight of Delmar Avenue, watched the activity on the crowded street and talked casually to each other. Music jumped out into the night from a local bar around the corner. People passed, paying little attention to the couple in the shadow of the apartment building. Three college students stumbled by as Phoenix continued to dispense shaving cream into the vents of the apartment's alarm system. Her hand holding the can, hidden by her body, continued to release the white foam that smelled of menthol into the vent until it overflowed. Small popping sounds were heard and Phoenix knew the system had short-circuited. She dropped the can into some dying bushes at the foot of the building then cleaned the excess foam from the vents with a spare piece of cloth. Phoenix winked at Dylan, gave him a kiss, then walked around to the back. Using her lock-pick set, she gently and quickly unlocked the back door. Thunder rumbled and rolled across the midwestern sky and Phoenix couldn't have hoped for a better night with Dylan.

"Wow, you're good."

"That's nothing," Phoenix said turning to Dylan. His walnut brown eyes, absorbing the faint light coming from inside the apartment, looked bigger, lighter in color than she remembered.

"Damn. I left the bag outside. Go on in, I'll be right back."

"This isn't some kinda game, ya know?"

Dylan kissed her. "Don't worry, baby, I'll be right back." Phoenix watched his lips form the words. When he turned to leave, she caught a glimpse of his profile and thought his brow and chin, even his nose, were in perfect symmetry.

Phoenix entered alone. Inside, she walked through the kitchen and received the apartment's impression. Every apartment had its own distinct feel, a sense of what the owners were like, what they've left behind in the dust of dead skin. She could immediately sense danger or tranquility. What she intuited from this place was a general feeling of calm. She looked toward the back door, waiting for Dylan. She quietly called out to him. She was about to go back outside when the doorbell rang.

"What the hell?"

The doorbell rang again and for a reason Phoenix couldn't explain, she decided not to run out and forget the whole thing; instead, she walked through the apartment to the front door. When she looked through the peephole, she saw Dylan standing there with his hair slightly wet from the rain that had started.

"Can Phoenix come out and play?" he asked when she opened the door. His white T-shirt stuck to his chest.

"Get in here," she said. "What a goof."

"He keeps his money in here," he said, walking down the dark hall. Phoenix watched him walk away, his legs pumping, and his ass tight under his jeans.

"This guy a friend of yours?" she asked, concerned about his willingness to rip off someone he knows.

Dylan turned to Phoenix. "Not a very good one," he said and kissed her.

Phoenix, immediately aroused, sexually engulfed, had to stop herself from biting into Dylan's chest and ripping of his T-shirt. She wrapped her leg around his, pulling him closer, feeling his crotch against her thigh. She pressed against him, feeling the wetness between her legs as she moved her hips. She ran her arms feverishly across Dylan's body.

When they separated, Dylan took a half step back and looked at Phoenix who breathed heavily through her mouth. He smiled and walked away.

"He keeps his money in here," he repeated.

"Flirt."

In the bedroom, Dylan rummaged around the dresser draws, discarding the contents onto the floor. When Phoenix entered the room, she saw the large bed by the window bathed in blue light, the sheets alive and moving from the rain reflecting off the window. In an instant Phoenix knew how this night was going to end. But as she was about to lay on the bed and wait for Dylan to stop ransacking the place, she saw something that made her forget all about him. In the corner, resting in its stand, sat a silver saxophone. The shadows from the Venetian blinds cut a diagonal line across the professional tenor sax. The falling rain softened and melted the image that shined in the night. Phoenix approached the instrument with reverence and sat beside it.

The saxophone had a light film of dust on it, and Phoenix used her shirt to clean it off. The mouthpiece and reed were still attached. She fingered the pads; they were good. While Dylan was looking for the money, Phoenix looked for the saxophone's case. When she found it in the closet she opened it and saw a blow-up doll wadded up inside. "Jeeeez."

"What?" Dylan asked.

Phoenix tossed the doll on the floor.

Dylan saw it and laughed. "I wish I could tell him we found that—talk about embarrassing!"

Phoenix went back to the sax, gently dissembled the instrument, and set it into its velvet cradle.

"Here it is! Dylan exclaimed, finding $2,100 in the bottom drawer under the socks. He always waits 'til he has over a $2,000 before he makes a deposit."

"This guy *is* a friend of yours," Phoenix said, disappointed in Dylan for stealing from someone he knows.

"He's not, really. He's a complete asshole, trust me."

Phoenix looked again at the blow-up doll. When she saw Dylan counting the money she said, "Don't count it now. Let's go."

"I told you, he'll be gone 'til tomorrow." Walking out the bedroom door, he added, "I have to pee. This kind of stuff makes me nervous."

The erotica of the night consumed Phoenix—finding the saxophone, the dance, the rain, the storm, and Dylan—she couldn't wait for him to be inside her, to feel herself wrapped around him. She wanted to merge with him, to burn with him. Standing by the window, Phoenix slowly undressed, touching herself, with the thought of Dylan touching her.

When Dylan returned, he saw her silhouetted in an ethereal glow from the window. Like a goddess, she stood, outlined in the distorted rain. Her shapely, unshaven legs, creating an almost aura-like haze that gave the impression of her floating. Dylan's eyes moved slowly up her shadowed pearl body. Her smooth, flat stomach had something shiny in the navel; it took Dylan a moment to realize it was pierced with silver. Her firm breasts and hard nipples were opalescent in the night's light. One breast was larger than the other and he'd never seen such perfection. Her hair rested on her shoulders and framed her face. Her full lips were slightly parted. Dylan wanted to crawl to Phoenix as he quietly vowed complete fidelity to his new religion.

Outside, the clouds that threatened a storm delivered their promise. The lightning and thunder arrived at the same time and the hard rain immediately flooded from the heavens. As the lightning shattered across the sky, the rain broke free from the wall of the thunderhead.

Inside, the sound of the saxophone played in Phoenix's mind as she started making love to Dylan. She heard the music, and Dylan's sounds of pleasure mingling with her own, creating an aria with the rain's quickening percussion and the sonorous thunder. Phoenix opened herself to the orchestra around her. Lightning illuminated the lovers and captured their intimate moments as a photograph. Their shadows fell on each other in a rolling landscape—Phoenix's hip, Dylan's thigh, the two moved in rhythm to the August storm outside. The wind started blowing harder, brushing tree limbs against the side of the building, scratching them against the window; their shadows, reaching out like arms, moved across the bodies of Dylan and Phoenix.

CHAPTER 9

Justin walked alone in the dark, deep in thought. He knew what Phoenix was doing. But it wasn't her dancing which saddened him: it was her dancing with Dylan. Breaking into places sexually aroused Phoenix—he didn't understand why, nor did she—but Justin knew if Phoenix broke into an apartment with a good-looking kid like Dylan, then at some point during the dance, or soon after, she'd be fucking him. The fact that she never seemed to be driven to fuck Justin during one of their dances disturbed him even more. He remembered catching her masturbating one night in a large department store where they were picking up kitchen appliances. That night Phoenix told him that breaking in made her horny and the story where she first discovered this strange titillation.

It was soon after she had moved to St. Louis after leaving New Orleans. She'd only planned to stay long enough to make some money before moving on, but she had no particular place to go and she was in no hurry to get there. Upon her arrival, Phoenix had found a hostel in Soulard and had stayed there for several weeks until she found a job as a waitress at a bar down the street.

One of the bartenders, an average looking man with unwarranted conceit, had let her stay with him while she saved money. One night, as they were driving home, he'd unexpectedly made a detour.

"Where are we going, Robert?"

"I thought we'd drop by Donny's and do some lines."

"Oh, okay."

When she had walked into Donny's apartment, she saw him sitting on his tattered couch, watching porno. "Hey, you brought her!"

Robert glared at him.

Donny's greeting sent a warning to Phoenix, and her observance of Robert's response had sealed the foreboding feeling. Robert turned to Phoenix and smiled, "Want a beer?"

"No thanks."

"Donny, cut us some lines, let's all loosen up a bit and have some fun," Robert said unconvincingly and sat down on the other end of the couch. "Have a seat, Phoenix," he patted the place between him and Donny.

"No, actually Robert, I think I'd like to go home."

"All right, let me do a few bumps first." Robert bent over to reach the fat line Donny had just cut in two quick strokes.

"Hey, Phoenix, you ever do that?" Donny asked, pointing to the threesome in the video.

"Can I use your phone?"

"Oh, come on Phoenix, lighten up. Donny's crude but he's okay, sit down."

"Are you taking me home, Robert, or should I start walking?"

"You *know*, Phoenix," Robert turned his head, "I let you stay at my crib for free, you could at least be sociable."

"How sociable, Robert?" Phoenix asked, her hand next to her butterfly knife tucked in her back pocket.

Donny laughed. "That sociable," he said, pointing to the TV with his remote and turning up the volume.

Phoenix looked at Robert who started to speak, "Shut up, Robert." She left, thankful they hadn't followed.

When Phoenix arrived at Robert's apartment, she'd realized she didn't have her keys with her. But like a prodigy, she'd suddenly realized its vulnerability. She'd noticed the hinges of the back door were on the outside, and although she never though about it before, she instinctively knew how she could get inside without keys. She'd pried up the rods that slip between the two sets of hinges and took the door off its frame. Her action had caused all her senses to become engorged and the night became full of sensuality. Later she would tell Justin their meeting was destined, because it was that first break-in—and the stimulation it produced—that put her on the path where she would meet him one night while breaking into his car.

Justin walked the tree-lined sidewalk of Soulard, past a corner house with stone lions at the gate, and recalled her trying to steal his car. "You'd have better luck with these," he had said, throwing his keys onto her lap. It had scared the shit out of her, he recalled, and laughed out in the deserted night. He turned the corner and started heading for J.B.'s. The storm had stopped an hour earlier and the night was cool and clean. Stars could be seen again and Justin felt their eyes upon him. In the dark, he passed a woman who smiled at him and asked him for a date, and a man who asked him for a dollar. Justin ignored both and returned to his thoughts about Phoenix.

One of their first dances had yielded over $10,000 in unsigned traveler's checks. They stayed up all night to be first in line when the bank opened, hoping the owners hadn't discovered their loss, hoping they got to the bank before their theft was reported. In the morning, Phoenix used her fake I.D. and cashed the checks in.

That night, to celebrate, Phoenix and Justin went out clubbing at a bar in East St. Louis. The dance music from groups like the Pet Shop Boys, Bronski Beat, and Duran Duran, pounded all night long and the alcohol, the cocaine, and the amyl nitrite drove the two well past sunrise.

In their apartment, as the new days sun lit upon the west wall a soft, orange glow, he kissed her. Her lips were soft and her mouth yielding. He imagined to be inside her would feel the same. He almost cried. He pulled her to him and held her softly. He caressed her face, looked into her eyes, pressed against her body. He wanted the moment chiseled in marble, caught in a photograph, captured in a painting. But then, unexpectedly, Phoenix pulled away.

"Justin, I can't do this, you're my best friend." She looked down, avoiding eye contact, obviously pained. "I value our friendship too much. It's too important to me. I don't want to risk that by fucking."

"I don't want to *fuck*. I want us to make love."

Phoenix looked up at him, "You want us to make *love?*"

"Yes."

"Oh, Justin..."

"What?"

"Make love? What are you saying? You're in love with me?"

"Yes."

"Oh, Justin... no." She looked away from him. "Don't be in love with me. Love me, but don't *be* in love with me. It'll change everything."

"No it won't."

"It already has," she said softly.

"Okay, so things will change," he said desperately. "What's wrong with that? Can't our relationship be better?"

"Justin, please." She turned away from him and quickly left.

Justin wanted to call out to her, to tell her to wait, to tell her to stop, but he knew he couldn't. Instead, he watched the door close behind her.

Justin Sunder didn't see her for several days. When she returned to Justin, he assured her it was the alcohol and drugs talking, and that he was caught up in the moment, and he was sorry if he made her feel uncomfortable, and he agreed they should remain friends. He'd spent the last year convincing her of that, convincing himself only in vain.

CHAPTER 10

After leaving the apartment, Phoenix and Dylan spent the next hour at a bar around the corner. A local band, Ultraman, was playing the driving punk rock that Phoenix thought contrasted perfectly with the soft and sensual night. Phoenix liked the band's rawness, Dylan liked their roughness, and the two stayed at the loud basement bar until the last note. After the bar closed, they drove down Delmar, talking and laughing comfortably with each other. At a small liquor store with bars on the windows and doors, Dylan bought a bottle of tequila, sliding his money through a hole cut in the bulletproof glass. They took turns taking shots as Phoenix made random turns throughout North St. Louis, past abandoned lots and burned out buildings, weeds and broken glass. Every now and then, in the midst of the darkness and decay, a restored townhouse would appear, painted and clean. The storm, which had passed while Phoenix and Dylan were inside the bar, gave the destitute, deserted area an illusion of cleansing, a hint of revival, a sense of what could be.

When they saw Grand Boulevard they followed it south and in 20 minutes they were approaching Tower Grove Park. Phoenix decided to cut through the 285 acres of Tower Grove Park, a former marshland that had thousands of selected trees planted throughout. They drove between the two griffins guarding the entrance, past the bronze statue of Shakespeare and the gazebos. The fragrances released from the rain permeated the park. The wet, shimmering road had little traffic. They passed one car as they merged around the circular intersection in the middle of the park and a single parked car by the Chinese shelter house.

Approaching the playground, they noticed a dozen kids clowning around with each other. When Dylan and Phoenix got closer, the teenagers stopped playing. As they drove past, several pulled out guns and held them to their chest, standing there like stone, waiting for the car to pass. At the other end of the park, they pulled onto Kingshighway and went to an art deco diner.

Dylan and Phoenix sat in the back in a booth upholstered in blue vinyl and talked casually like old friends. The waitress, wearing a '50s bouffant hairstyle, took their orders without writing it down. After she walked away, Phoenix noticed five friends of her and Justin's enter, squinting their eyes in the bright fluorescent lamps of the diner. Phoenix called them over and all seven squeezed together into the booth. The additions to Phoenix and Dylan's party placed their orders, and when the food came, the company shared each other's plates. Dylan easily ingratiated himself with Phoenix's friends by simply just listening.

Afterward, Carl, a redhead with alabaster skin who wore his hairstyle like Caesar, suggested they go back to his place to continue their impromptu party. They all agreed. Dylan offered to pay the bill and Phoenix smiled. "You're just loaded with etiquette, ain't cha?" she said and winked.

Carl lived in an immaculately preserved Victorian townhouse in Lafayette Square across from the haunted, abandoned Lafayette Park with an eccentric woman three times his age who spent most of her time overseas. The large rooms throughout the three-story house were usually unlit and filled with things the woman brought back with her. Shadows of large paintings, crates, statues, and furniture littered the rooms.

The party climbed the winding, ornate, wooden and marble staircase to the second floor "party room," the only room lit in the entire house. Everybody sat down while Carl went into the kitchen for drinks. Joannie, an overweight 19-year-old who, in Dylan's opinion, talked too much, lit up a joint and passed it around. Skinny and silent Phillip, who wore his makeup poorly, his nose and forehead always shining, cut some lines from his gram of coke. Oversexed Stephanie and her new boy, Tony, were high on ex-tacy and hardly knew there were other people around.

Later that night, during a lull in the conversation, Phoenix overheard Tony telling Stephanie something that made her listen with hidden intent: "The dude had a stack of hundreds three feet high," Tony said, thinking he was only speaking to Stephanie but talking loud enough for Phoenix to easily eavesdrop. "I couldn't believe it. There I was and he was counting a C-note every second for twenty minutes, man, the dude is fat!"

"Who is this guy?" Stephanie asked.

"His name is David. He's like, *thee* man. He's a friend of mine. I've been hanging with him for a couple of months now, I'll introduce you to him."

"I think I know him... tall guy, dresses like a preppy?"

"Yeah, his shirts are always starched, man."

"Yeah, his friend tried to pick me up one night."

"That'd be Kevin. Big guy, goatee, black-framed glasses?"

"Yeah, that's him."

When Dylan heard the description of Kevin he thought about the incident at J.B.'s. He turned to Tony, intending to interject something into their conversation, but Phoenix tapped his arm, held up a finger, and shook her head.

"Does he have a loft downtown?" Stephanie asked, unaware that Phoenix was listening.

Tony nodded his head, "On Washington, a huge penthouse condo."

"I think I was at a party there once," Stephanie said.

Tony continued to try to impress Stephanie about David and talked about him for another half hour. By the end of the conversation, Phoenix knew exactly where David lived and even where they might find his stash.

Finally, Tony and Stephanie left for one of the six bedrooms. Carl invited everyone to spend the night. He then excused himself and followed the couple into the bedroom. A few minutes later Carl came running out, laughing, and carrying a Polaroid camera with three photos documenting the amorous act of Stephanie and Tony. When he knew they were well into the act, he motioned the party to follow him.

"Boy, they picked the wrong room," he said mischievously. "Look at this." Carl pointed to a two-way mirror he'd recently installed. There, for all to view, were Stephanie and Tony having sex.

"You have to stand still," Carl informed the party. "Otherwise they'll see us."

Phoenix and Dylan watched for a while and then decided to leave when it looked like Stephanie was going to give Tony a golden shower.

"Man, not on the bed! Those sick bastards!" Tony protested.

Phoenix laughed, "Jeez, Carl, what else do you have in this den of iniquity?"

"Hey, the old woman is kinky. What can I say?"

On the way out the door Dylan said, "You know, I'm just a good ol' boy from the South Side and that was all just too weird."

"Was it?"

CHAPTER 11

Phoenix drove Dylan home. The sun opened the horizon and bathed them in its light as they drove east. Rarely did Phoenix miss the sun's rise. She looked radiant in the sun's fire like she belonged in it, her eyes sparkling, her face smooth like a calm ocean at dawn. When Dylan suggested he spend the night with her, Phoenix declined his proposition.

"Is there something going on between you and your roommate—what's his name? Justin?"

Phoenix smiled. "No."

"I just want to know, that's all."

"No, he's my friend, Dylan. I like you. Don't get possessive on me now."

Dylan remembered being introduced as a friend tonight and suddenly "friend" took on a whole new meaning for him. He wondered if Justin was the same kind of *friend* that he was. *Phoenix and Justin*, he thought, *she lives with him, there's gotta be something going on.*

They arrived at Dylan's two-story house that he shared with his father and made plans to see each other again. Phoenix watched him walk the inclined driveway. Before she left, she honked her horn. Law, Dylan's bull terrier inside the house, immediately started barking when he heard the horn but stopped as soon as he recognized his master's presence at the side door. The only light on was in the living room, which could be seen from the road. Leroy Panicosky, Dylan's father, always left the living room light on.

The house itself had gone through little change over the past twenty-five years. Dylan remembered the kitchen, the carpet, the wallpaper, even the workbench in the corner of the basement; all looked the same as they did in his youth. Nevertheless, the house was not the same. The way it *felt* was different. Since the death of his mother and brother, it was an apparition of a house. His father, who used to embrace life, had changed dramatically after the loss of his wife and son. Leroy Panicosky used to challenge life and enjoy all it had to offer. He used to take chances simply to feel the rush of life as he teased it. *Loving life* is what he called it. After Billy died and then a year later Rachel, Leroy Panicosky stopped talking about his days as a biker. He refused to speak of the days when he rode his Harley with his friends, men he served with in World War II who formed a club but never bothered giving it a name. In the late '40s, he and his veteran pals would get together for rides and stay away for months at a time. Leroy used to tell Dylan the stories from the road and the sights he'd seen: the Grand Canyon, the Rocky Mountains, the Atlantic Ocean, Death Valley, Yellowstone Park. In South Dakota, Leroy met an old Sioux Indian who, as a 20-year-old brave, had fought against Custer. He had been to the infant casinos in Las Vegas and lost a whole month's salary of $80. He had witnessed the country's push to provide housing after the war with subdivisions sprouting up everywhere. In the early '50s, he, his friends, and his new bride saw the country from their motorcycles; he saw the deserts, the lakes, the mountains; and he saw the factories, the cities, and the farms.

But now, after losing his wife and son, Leroy also seemed to lose his interest in life. He worked, he ate, and he slept. He fed and walked Law, and he watched TV. On Friday nights, he got drunk. And even though he couldn't find it in himself to sell his motorcycle, he refused to ride it anymore. Leroy's bike, covered by a thick, gray tarp, sat quietly in the garage corner next to Billy's; his father's Harley, draped like a tombstone, sat next the grave of his son's.

Dylan Panicosky had lived in the same house practically all his life, except for the time he had spent in prison for involuntary manslaughter.

He wasn't a violent man but on rare occasions Dylan would lose control and his anger would take over. The night he killed a man was one of those times. He and his brother were walking down the street when someone in a passing car yelled out: "Fucking hoosiers!" —A pejorative in St. Louis dating back to the '30s where scab workers from Indiana were brought in to fill in for strikers. A full beer can, hitting Billy in the neck, followed the insult. Billy grabbed the can and threw it back at the car, cracking the rear window. The car stopped and four men got out.

"Look what you did to my window, you motherfucker!"

The brawl began the moment Billy reached the driver, no words, no gesticulating, no threats. Billy fought with the skills of a trained warrior, Dylan like a berserker Viking. The enraged lust for blood surged through Dylan when he saw all four passengers jump on his brother. He was pummeling a guy when Billy dragged him off. His lawyers, paid for by Billy the Kid's motorcycle club, pleaded self-defense due to them being outnumbered, temporary insanity in the face of perceived impending death, and asked for leniency due to the innocence of his age and sincere remorse, He spent a year locked up until his appeal was granted and was released.

Dylan walked into his house and was met by Law; his powerful, light brown dog wagged its broken tail in greeting. Law, a beloved member of the family, when there was a family, licked Dylan's chin. Before Dylan went to prison, before his brother was murdered, before his mother had died, before his father had lost his will to live, there was Law.

Dylan's father, Leroy Panicosky, taught Law how to ride on the back of his Harley. Dylan's mother, Rachel, spoiled Law, taking him everywhere with her, and protested profusely when Billy wanted to train the dog to attack. In the end, Billy won. Just before Dylan's appeal, Law got into a fight with a neighbor's Doberman twice Law's size. When the neighbor, only trying to scare the dogs apart and stop them from fighting, shot at them, he accidentally hit Law's tail. After Dylan's release, when he asked about his dogs permanently bent tail, the Panicoskys told him a different story.

Once inside the house, Dylan playfully rubbed Law's head with both hands and gave his pet a kiss on the nose. While cleaning up after his father, Dylan thought about Phoenix and Justin. He was surprised at the slight surge of jealousy he felt toward Justin so soon after meeting Phoenix. *Ah, but Phoenix*, he thought, *every man must want her.*

"I got to protect me and mine, eh Law?" Dylan grabbed Law's chew toy and tossed it down the hall. When Law came running back, Dylan tripped over him and landed into the wall, dropping the plate he was carrying. "Law, ya son of a bitch!" While Dylan was bent over, picking up the broken plate, Law wagged his tail and licked Dylan's face. "Okay, okay," he said between licks. "Damn dog," he said and tossed the chew toy again.

CHAPTER 12

Phoenix walked into her loft and saw Justin sitting there reading a book. He put it down as soon as she walked in.

"What are you still doing up?" she asked.

"Well, when your body gets used to staying up 'til dawn, it's hard to break its rhythm."

That morning she told Justin about Dylan—omitting the sex in the apartment—the saxophone, running into their friends and then the party at Carl's, where she got into more details about her night.

"Apparently, he's some big coke dealer with connections in Columbia."

"Columbia? Are you saying he's connected to fucking Escobar?"

"Could just be a rumor to keep people out."

"Damn."

"He's a big fish in a little pond. He's got some kid, Tony, working for him mouthing off shit, how discerning can he be? I mean, he told us that David keeps his cash in the master bathroom for god's sake. What kind of a player leaks that kind of information to an underling?"

"A confidant and arrogant one? Someone who's testing this new underling?"

"Let's just check it out. We'll get high and pull some surveillance, gather Intel, get some proper burglary gear like night goggles and zip lines." She offered a coquettish look. "It'll be fun."

Justin grinned. "You're gonna be the death of me."

"I'd give my life for you," Phoenix said seriously.

"Me, too."

She went to kitchen and came back with two large bottles of imported beer. When she returned she asked if Dylan could come along.

"Phoenix, we don't know anything about this guy."

"He's cool, I'm telling you. It'll be okay, trust me."

"Just because you danced with him tonight doesn't mean anything. It could have been a setup."

"Oh, you're paranoid, Justin. Have I ever been wrong about following my instincts?"

"Well, no, you do have a sixth sense when it comes to that sort of thing."

"Then trust me on this one, will you?" Phoenix pulled a cigarette out of her silver cigarette case, tapped it twice and by the time she had it in her mouth, Justin had a light for her.

"I don't know, Phoenix, Dylan is good looking and all that," he said scratching his scar, an unconscious gesture that Phoenix observed. "But, we've done so well on our own. We don't need to make an organized ring of it all; we don't need to start recruiting people."

"We're not, honey." Phoenix sat next to Justin. "We're just bringing him along for the ride."

Justin tried to control his jealousy. Was he really worried about Dylan or was he just trying to keep him away from Phoenix?

"He can drive the getaway car."

"But I drive the getaway car," Justin joked.

"I think you'll like him, Justin, give him a chance. He's not as intelligent as you but he's not stupid. Tonight, when Stephanie was talking about how this country seemed to be turning increasingly to television and stupid sit-coms to laugh away their problems, Dylan said that the masses need an escape, and the powerful will always find room in their budget to fund distractions."

"Okay, so he has some insight."

"Then he pointed out the window and said 'squirrel.'"

Justin laughed, and knew he'd have to adapt. *After all*, Justin thought, *who was he to deny or try to jeopardize her happiness?* So, Justin, against his better judgment and fighting his feelings of jealousy, agreed to Phoenix's request of bringing Dylan along to a dance.

Phoenix, pleased with Dylan and wanting to please Justin, picked up her saxophone and started playing. Standing by the window, Phoenix caressed the first notes. They came labored at first, but as she retrained her fingers, regained her embouchure, and relearned her breathing technique, her ability and talent returned. She had forgotten how much she enjoyed playing. Phoenix, wrapped in the white light of morning, felt reborn.

As she played, she thought of Horatius Alastair.

Horatius had been the first gentleman Phoenix ever knew. A tall Scot with a balding head and a passion for chivalry. He saw Phoenix as a damsel in distress and did everything he could for the falling angel. He taught music at Juilliard and had offered her a place to stay when she was 15. They had met at a party one night that one of Horatius' students was throwing -- a graduation party that Phoenix crashed with a friend of hers. Professor Alastair and Phoenix had talked all night, and even though it wasn't Phoenix's style to offer any information that might show her destitution, Horatius picked up on her need and innocently offered her lodging at his apartment on the Upper-West Side. During her stay, he'd taught her how to play the saxophone. He never forced himself upon her nor demanded anything from her other than dedication.

"Phoenix," he said one morning when she came crawling in. "We had a lesson an hour ago."

"I know, Harry. I'm sorry, but the night just wouldn't end."

"Don't blame it on Apollo. You didn't have to wait for the sun to come home."

"Can we do it now?"

"No, I've a class to teach. I'll see you later. If you want, the lesson is waiting for you over there."

He left, and Phoenix, fighting sleep, picked up the sax and played the lesson he left for her. She played it now for Horatius and also for Justin.

Listening to Phoenix, Justin wondered where—when—she had learned to play so well.

CHAPTER 13

The buildings of downtown St. Louis fascinated Justin; it was the only city west of the Mississippi that had any respectable turn of the century architecture. He would often spend the early hours just before the golden sunset admiring the old buildings. As Justin waited for the moon to call the noctimaniacs and the nightwalkers, he would drive or walk the empty St. Louis city streets and marvel at the different architectural designs and styles displayed in the old buildings: the Romanesque Union Station, the Second Empire-style of the Old Post Office, the Paris Hotel de Ville-inspired City Hall. In the Garment District—a once thriving metropolis 100 years ago but now practically a ghost town—Justin looked at the impressive structures of Greek Revival that still remained. However, like most of the nocturnal people who walked the deserted city streets, these buildings were only shells.

Recently, in an attempt to revive the area, the name had been changed to the Loft District, and several developers had started renovating a few of the empty brick warehouses into condominiums, apartments and artist studios. In one of these buildings sat David's condominium. Phoenix, Dylan, and Justin were in a stolen car creeping down Washington Avenue to the apartment Stephanie and Tony had talked about. Justin, driving the getaway car and acting as the lookout, drove to the dance somewhat disappointed. Several factors added to his feeling of ostracization: Dylan, who was friendly but reserved toward Justin, claimed ownership of Phoenix early in the evening by his display of affection; and Phoenix, whose attention was mostly directed to Dylan, further removed Justin; and lastly, a strange feeling Justin had toward the dance in general. In fact, Justin cared little about dancing any more. But he promised to help Phoenix so there he was listening to Dylan talk about the city.

"My grandpa worked there when he was thirteen, making shoelaces," Dylan said pointing to the empty International Shoe Company building. "Hung himself after my dad was born."

"What?" Phoenix asked.

"Yeah, my dad and I used to come here to shop in the old Famous Bar when I was a kid. He told me all kinds of stories. The saloon story about Stagger Lee happened just around the corner past Tucker."

"Stagger Lee, I've heard those songs. That was real?" Justin said.

"Yeah, it's a blues standard, I think. Everybody's covered it. Up here is where my mom met my dad," Dylan said, pointing to an unkempt parking lot. Phoenix and Justin looked at each other. "No, it used to be some soda-fountain place."

Phoenix laughed, "That's good."

"You know that song 'Frankie and Johnny'," Dylan asked. "Elvis covered it? They actually lived in an apartment where the Opera house sits.

"St. Louis has an opera house?"

"I think it's closed," Dylan said.

"Like everything else in this town."

When Justin found the address, he pulled around back and let Phoenix and Dylan out at the corner.

"Hurry up and be careful," Justin said then drove up the brick-paved alley where he watched Phoenix and Dylan walk to the loading dock like they lived there. Driving on the old bricks provided by demolished buildings, Justin wondered how they ended up in the ground, what type of designs had been destroyed, how many beautiful buildings with so much promise had fallen to end up as an alley?

As Phoenix used her lock-pick to get through the door, Justin looked at the seven-story building looming overhead. *So much history,* he thought, *probably built in the late 1800s.* The red brick building with its massive, chiseled pink granite was unique. He wanted to be inside; he wanted to see the interior. He hoped the developers found a way to complement the existing design and keep the old building's integrity. Justin had seen too many buildings become sterilized by the renovators slapping dry-wall up every 20 square feet installing quasi-modern kitchens decorated all in stainless steel and laying industrial gray wall-to-wall carpet.

Looking up at the building, his eyes were drawn to another old building being renovated. The wooden window frames had been replaced by bright white aluminum storm windows that shone even in the dead of night, breaking up the building's design, and the buildings around it by its vagrant display of modernization. In the clear September night a few clouds were pushed across the sky and the whiteness of the clouds seemed to reflect off the white window frames; the full moon, too, shone brightly off them. Justin saw how the other buildings belonged, how they merged with each other and the night, where as this one boldly did not. It was a simple thing—the storm windows—but it represented so much more to Justin. These people would tear down four beautiful buildings to accommodate parking for one skyscraper. *There's no connection to the past*, he thought, *no respect for it.*

Justin mused over the inability of businessmen to look past the immediate dollar when suddenly his eyes were pulled down seven floors to the alley. Car lights could be seen coming down a side street. He quickly looked to the door by the loading dock—Phoenix and Dylan should have been inside by now, but they were still there. By the time the car pulled around the corner, the two were embraced with Phoenix's back against the door. The rouse was routine. Phoenix and Justin had embraced before to hide their intentions, but this time it wasn't Justin holding onto Phoenix for a fleeting moment; it wasn't his body her arms were around; it wasn't his lips she kissed, or his cheeks. As soon as the car turned the corner, Phoenix pushed against the door with her body, removed herself from Dylan's kiss, and stepped backwards into the doorway. Justin watched Phoenix beckon Dylan inside.

While waiting for Phoenix and Dylan, Justin looked at a newer, utilitarian building down the street and thought again about how it didn't fit in. *No connection to the past*, he thought again. The newer building reminded him of his father and when he turned away to look at the aesthetically more pleasing architecture of an older building his thoughts turned to his mother. *No respect for the past.* A seed of an idea starting forming in the visage of his mother's brother, George Sitting Wolf. The more he thought about the past, the more his thoughts became focused on his maternal family's past, his uncle's past, *his* past, *his* history. The dark mountains of brick and steel surrounding him dissolved into a landscape of rolling hills where a vision of his uncle George Sitting Wolf seemed to be waiting.

CHAPTER 14

Inside the converted warehouse, Phoenix and Dylan climbed the back staircase seven flights, each landing painted a different color. On the red level, they found the door to the condominium owned by someone they only knew as David. It was midnight on a Friday night, and they knew he'd be gone for at least four more hours. The condo was silent behind the locked door. In fact, the entire building was eerily still which engorged Phoenix's senses. She felt like she'd be able to smell the alcohol on the breath of a drunk coming up the elevator. She picked David's lock and walked in.

But once inside her initial excitement turned to dread. She immediately sensed the danger lodged in that loft. She looked back at the door hoping to see Justin walk through. She left the door slightly ajar and reluctantly entered further into David's lair. Dylan was confident but ignorant of what they just walked into. Justin was right: Dylan was too inexperienced. Phoenix went to a window to see if she could see Justin. She thought she'd try to signal him up somehow, she wondered why they had never bought walkie-talkies. But David's windows faced away from the alley. She thought about going back to get him. *If Justin was here*, she said to herself, *it would be okay—no, Phoenix, finish the job. Don't waste any more time. You can do this.*

Dylan went to a David's entertainment wall that held dozens of various electronic devices. From the audio system, speakers, reel-to-reel, to the large-screen TV, VCR, and camcorder, David had every modern day distraction money could buy. Dylan started unplugging equipment.

"Leave that shit alone, we can't carry all that," she said, collecting her thoughts, and quickly left for the bathroom where David kept his money. *God, I hope that kid was right.*

"I can get 400 bucks for that thing alone," Dylan said, pointing to a high quality camcorder sitting on a tripod. Damn. We're gonna have to come back with a truck for the rest of this stuff," he said, looking at all the toys in David's condo.

"Trust me, leave everything alone," she called out to him from the bathroom. "I wanna get the fuck outta here."

Phoenix opened every door, slid open every panel, kicked baseboards, tapped on drywall, moved photos, lifted, pushed and pulled on everything she could find. "This was a fuckin' stupid fuckin' idea," she kept saying to herself. She was about to give up but decided to pull everything out from under the sink to see if there was a trap door of sorts. When she tossed an unusually heavy eight-pack of toilet paper onto the slate floor, several 100 dollar bills fluttered loose. Phoenix closed her eyes and let out a sigh that sounded to Dylan like an orgasm.

"Hey, baby, don't start without me," he said, walking down the hall.

Phoenix grabbed the cleverly disguised toilet paper rolls and shoved them in her oversized bag. She then put everything back the way she found it and started out. She was met at the doorway by Dylan and screamed.

Dylan laughed, "Jesus, baby, take it easy, it's just me. I have to pee. This kind of thing—"

"I know, makes you nervous."

Dylan smiled and kissed her.

"But hurry up," she said pulling away. "We gotta go. Mission accomplished."

"Damn, you are good."

While standing by the back door, she calculated the score to be easily over $20,000. Her hands were sweating when Dylan finally returned carrying the camcorder. "Take that back, Dylan. Goddamn it, take it back!"

Dylan planted his foot between her legs, his thigh pressing against hers. "What's the big deal? Do you think he's gonna give a shit his camcorder was stolen after what you just grabbed?" He grinded against her in a circular motion. "How much did we get anyway?"

Phoenix stepped back. "This is serious, Dylan. Put it back and let's get the hell out of here!"

Dylan looked closer at Phoenix. "What's wrong with you?"

"If this dude comes home and sees that somebody just danced in his apartment, the first thing he's going to do is go to his stash."

"So?"

"So, if nothing's disturbed he may not even go in there for a couple of days. That buys us time. If only his cash is gone, he'll think someone he knows took it; he won't even look for us; we're strangers to him. Take it back and let's go!"

"Okay, okay, I can do this. Professionalism, right? No problem. But I think I gotta pee again—"

"Dylan!"

"Just kidding, geez. Go on, I'll catch up."

"Okay, I'll see you outside." She gave him a kiss and turned to leave. "Don't forget to hook everything back up," she said and started down the stairs.

Outside, Justin looked at his watch and started the stolen station wagon, letting it idle while he waited. A minute later the back door opened and Phoenix emerged. Justin put the car in gear and slowly drove toward her. By the time he reached her, Dylan came bounding out the back door and ran to catch up with her. They jumped in the car and Justin started to drive off.

"Wait, Justin, stop the car."

"Now? Now's not the time."

"I was thinking about something Phoenix said."

Phoenix looked at Dylan. "What I say? Forget it, now's not the time."

"No, no, no, just wait a second. Stop the car."

Justin pulled over to the curb.

"We want everything to be left alone, right?"

"Yes."

"Then why did we take the toilet paper rolls? Shouldn't we leave that behind, too?"

Justin looked at Phoenix. "Toilet paper rolls?"

Phoenix opened her bag.

"Hmm."

"He's got a point," she said.

"Yep, he's right," Justin, said, putting the car in park.

"Come on doll face," Dylan said, "we're going back in!"

"I'm not going back in there," Phoenix said. "Justin, would you?"

"What's it like?"

"A breeze. Two simple locks. The back staircase is deserted, you could be in and out in five minutes."

Justin watched Phoenix's face as she unpacked the bills from the rolls. His mind raced to the possibilities of her trepidation to return to David's loft. Secretly, he hoped Dylan had fucked up, but he doubted it as his suggestion to return the toilet paper was a solid one.

"He's gonna need those when he finds his stash gone," Dylan said, and Phoenix smiled.

After Justin and Dylan left, Phoenix thought about Dylan wanting to return the toilet paper; it was a minor detail but important. She was proud he made that call, and a little embarrassed she had missed it.

Phoenix jumped over to the driver's side and counted the money... $40,000 dollars. She divided it up three ways with the extra bill going to Dylan's pile. When her two men returned she drove the station wagon back to Dogtown, a working class municipality on the edge of the city famous for being the highest point in St. Louis. She parked the car five houses down from where Justin had stolen it, leaving a full tank for the owner and questions in the morning as to how it got there. She snickered as the imaginary scenario of tomorrow morning played out in her head: *I wasn't drunk, Martha, I parked the car right there in the back! Sure you did, John, that's why it's in O'Malley's front yard. I'm telling you, it's those damn kids!*

Phoenix jumped in the back seat of Justin's car and snuggled up to Dylan. Justin watched them in his rearview mirror.

"Should I take you two back to Dylan's?" Justin asked Phoenix as if to say: Please don't bring him home, I couldn't take it.

Phoenix looked at Justin, then Dylan.

"If you don't mind," Dylan said to Phoenix, "I wouldn't mind going home alone. I gotta drive my dad out to Jeff City in the morning, and I'm kinda beat."

"Okay, baby."

"I did good tonight?" Dylan asked with a sly smile.

"You did good tonight."

"See, I told ya."

Justin hit play on the cassette player to drown out their conversation. When *Sex* by Berlin started pulsating through the speakers, Justin just shook his head.

"Good choice, Justin."

"Shut up, Dylan."

Phoenix laughed and gave Justin a kiss on his cheek.

CHAPTER 15

"You like this boy."

"Yeah."

"Okay."

"You?"

"I don't know," Justin said, opening a bottle of wine.

"I'm very happy right now; with you, and now him, I'm just so very happy."

"Are you sure he's worth it?"

"Yeah, he could use a little help, a little polishing, but yeah, I think he is." Phoenix held up her glass, which Justin promptly filled. "Will you help him?"

Justin splashed the red wine into his glass. "To 40,000!" he said, lightly touching Phoenix's glass.

"Cheers."

They each took a sip of their Shiraz while looking into each other's eyes.

"You really like him, huh?"

"Yes, I do."

"Then I'll do what I can, for you," Justin said as he rose and walked to the indoor garden in the corner.

"Thanks." Phoenix said to Justin's back as he stepped on the woodchips that cracked under his feet.

"You don't mind?" She called out to him.

"What?" Justin asked, looking at the row of cacti beginning to lose their flowers.

"Dylan being around."

"No," Justin said as he pushed his fingers into the needles of the nearest cactus.

"Good," Phoenix said walking over to join Justin at the garden. "You know, I was thinking about this David character and I have to wonder... what kind of person has forty thousand bones just laying around?"

"He's a dealer. He can't deposit too much money. The IRS, DEA, the FBI—all of them keeps track of large cash deposits."

"Maybe," Phoenix thought aloud, pushing aside the crepe de Chine curtains that billowed in the breeze from the open window, separating her from Justin, "Maybe, on this one, we shouldn't have brought Dylan."

"I think you're right."

"But still, 40,000, not bad for one night's work, eh?" She asked, feeling isolated in Justin's garden.

"No."

Phoenix nodded and walked away.

On a wooden table just beyond the garden's rock perimeter sat Phoenix's saxophone. She picked up the case and went into her bedroom. Justin listened to her playing as he reflected over recent events, specifically the image of his uncle who appeared amidst the debris of downtown St. Louis. How did the life he had expected taken such a dramatic turn? And was it worth it any more? *It was never meant to go this far.*

At Washington University he had a friend obsessed with security systems.

"With every single system invented," his friend had said, "there are two ways to get around it. There's always a flaw—it can't be avoided; it's intrinsic," he told Justin one night. "I'm going to invent a system that can't be breached."

Through their conversations his friend inadvertently disclosed the Achilles' heel in every possible alarm system devised by man. And Justin used his new knowledge soon after the last conversation he had with his parents when they talked about their neighbor's upcoming Christmas party.

The Ladons were especially rude to Justin after the accident. His scar, the long hair he grew in an attempt to conceal it, the dark, turtleneck shirts he wore to help him hide the defect, and the change in his behavior and attitude were considered extremely unattractive by the Ladons. They even went so far as to exclude him from their annual Christmas party because, they said, "Some people might be offended." His parents agreed and suggested that he stay in St. Louis with his new friends, most of who had already left for the holidays to spend time with their families.

"Of course, you can come home. We'd love to have you here," his mother had said over the phone. "It's just that Margot and Lee haven't made provisions for an extra guest."

"What does their party have to do with me?"

"Nothing, sweetheart, nothing at all. It's just that Daddy and I are going to be at the party and we don't want you to be alone."

"So, you're saying I should stay in St. Louis?"

"Only until after the party, dear."

"You're telling me I should *not* come home until after the Ladon's party?"

"We're not saying that."

"Then I'm coming home."

"That's fine, Justin, come home, but if you do anything to jeopardize our relationship with the Ladons your father and me are going to be very upset with you. We've worked really hard to build this important contact, and we don't want you showing—well, just showing up and getting all melodramatic on us about—well, it's just that you've become so unpredictable lately, we don't know what to expect from you anymore."

They continued to argue for a while. His father, via speakerphone, joined the conversation and attempted to help his wife skirt the real issue: that of their son's mutilation, and their allegiance to people made uncomfortable over his defacement. Justin hung up and decided there was no real reason to ever talk to them again. They only reached out to him once after that: when they heard he dropped out of Wash U.

On New Year's Eve, he drove to Kansas City and broke into the Ladon's home. He knew they would be with his parents at Times Square, celebrating the arrival of 1984. The alarm was easily skirted by taking a glasscutter and creating a hole just above the latch that locked the window. The simple system, only equipped to handle the forced entry of broken glass that compromised the electronic security tape, offered no obstacle. Once the latch was slid out of place, he raised the window.

Inside he turned on the stereo and danced around by himself at a party that ended several days before.

"A simply delightful party, Mrs. Ladon. Well, thank you, my dear; we did our best to invite just the right people. Oh, heavens yes! More eggnog? Oh, no, I've had too much already—Ha-Ha-Ha! We can't allow the wife of an important senator to have eggnog on her face—Ha-Ha-Ha!"

Justin didn't know that in the very room he now danced in, both his parents had shook the hand of the malignant surgeon responsible for his scar and even offered their apologies for their lawsuit against him.

After the accident, his parents had called in Dr. Veli, not because of his expertise but because he was the doctor used by the people with which they wished to surrounded themselves. Dr. Veli assured them that a skin graft would replace the burned tissue, and after the scars from the surgery healed, nobody would even know he had acne, let alone a burn. The skin graft didn't work, and the result was the scar he now carried with as much dignity as he could. They lost the malpractice suit against Dr. Veli. Despite the evidence in the before-and-after pictures, which Dr. Veli intended to use to show his talents to patients who wanted cosmetic surgery, they lost at every level. Dr. Veli had more wealth, influence, and power than his parents. At the party, they shook hands and buried the hatchet. Later that night, Dr. Veli agreed to let Nathan Sunder design his new house.

Justin didn't know what he was doing in the Ladons' mansion. He didn't want anything; he didn't know what to take. He looked around, picking up things and dropping them. In the library, he took their complete collection of first edition Hemingway's. In the den, he took a stapler. In the wine cellar he grabbed a bottle of Gran Reserva from Spain and a bottle of Barbaresco from Italy, thinking even their best wines were mediocre. In the master bedroom, he took Mrs. Ladon's vibrator. When he saw Mr. Ladon's 9mm automatic Beretta, still loaded with 20 rounds in its clip, he took that too and finally left. Justin took his booty and, with the stereo still playing, walked out the front door. He crossed the secluded, private street to his parent's house and got into his car.

He'd been dancing now for three years and he started to question the validity of what he was doing. Did he really want to be a thief anymore? He loved Phoenix, but he wasn't sure if he was capable of keeping up with her lifestyle. Justin had to re-evaluate many things: his relationship with his family, his motivation to become a thief, his relationship with Phoenix, and this new guy who came from nowhere.

As Phoenix played her saxophone, Justin wanted to go to her and hold her but instead went to his bedroom, falling asleep with Phoenix through her music. Before sleep took him, he imagined his lips on the reed of her mouth, his hands caressing her neck, playing her body.

CHAPTER 16

The opulent wealth displayed on the private streets of the city's Central West End reminded Justin of the West Bank in Kansas City. The houses in his hometown didn't have the character, or the history, the St. Louis houses did, but the memories were the same. Memories he tried to isolate and control.

That night, driving to the dance in the West End, Phoenix had Dylan with her, and Justin felt like a stranger. As much as Justin hated to admit it, he actually liked Dylan. He liked him for several reasons but most importantly he liked Dylan's character, something that can't be defined by the cut of one's clothes or lineage. The way he presented himself was honest and genuine, without conceit, and that made him easy to talk to.

Phoenix drove down an alley that allowed them to see their mark two streets over between the houses lined 20 yards apart.

"The one with the cupola, there, see it?" Justin said to Phoenix, pointing.

"Got it."

"Okay, drop us off and come back here and wait for us to signal, and we'll see you at the back door."

"Let's do it," Phoenix said, turning the wheel. She pulled the stolen Lincoln into the driveway and stopped at the circular drive behind the house. "See you soon." She kissed Dylan then Justin as they each got out. Using the car as a shield, they ran bent over to the back door where they stayed hidden in its shadows. Phoenix continued around the circular drive and headed back out.

"What's a cupola?" Dylan asked as Justin began disarming the alarm system.

"The round room on top of the roof. You'll see it later because that's where we're going to turn on the light to let Phoenix know we're ready."

"We're going to climb all the way upstairs and turn on a light?"

Justin smiled. "Yep, and we're going to keep it on, too."

"Why don't we just light a flare?"

"Don't worry about it, Dylan. It's after we've taken what we wanted. We'll be fine. We turn on the light, run downstairs and Phoenix meets us in the back driveway."

"Shouldn't we be more careful?"

"Entering is the biggest risk. We got that down; getting in is no problem. Once we're in, staying away from open windows and wearing gloves are our only concerns, no problem there." He held up a gloved hand. Dylan looked down at his covered hands. "Once the dance is over," Justin continued, "we casually drive off, quietly ditch the car and drive home. A lantern on in the belvedere, like a beacon, is only a calling card; sure, it's dramatic, but what the hell. On this one," he paused, remembering the conflicting teachings at David's, "once the damage is done, it doesn't matter. It all depends on the dance, ya know?"

"Yeah, I get it."

"Okay, the alarm is off. Your turn."

They walked over to the back door where Justin handed Dylan his lock-pick set. Standing behind him, holding a folded duffel bag, Justin watched Dylan use the tools he was earlier trained with to attempt his first break-in.

"Lift it up 'til you feel it catch."

"I know."

"Now turn."

"I know."

The lock clicked. "You got it!"

"I know, will you stop!"

Justin smiled at him and winked. Dylan opened the door. "After you."

Unseen by Dylan and Justin, Phoenix sat on the hood of the car, smoking a cigarette. A police siren was heard in the distance.

"Shit!" Dylan said, running to the window when he heard the sirens wail several blocks away.

"Relax and get away from the window. It's the ones you don't hear you have to worry about."

Dylan reluctantly moved back into the deep shadows of the house and followed Justin into the living room. "You make this shit up as you go?" Dylan asked. From the light of the moon, he saw furniture that impressed him: large Victorian antique-like settees, chairs, and sofas. "Wow, look at this place."

"Shit," Justin said adamantly. "It's all shit for the bourgeoisie who think they have style."

Dylan pointed out the elaborate chairs covered in embroidered velvet. "This is nice stuff, man."

"It's gaudy. It's outdated furniture designed in the 1700s for women wearing large, cumbersome hoops. It belongs in a museum."

"You really are a pretentious bastard, aren't you?"

"Not at all. But that is," he said pointing at a large oil painting over the fireplace mantle of what could only be a portrait of the owner of the house.

"What are you doing? You're passing up some great stuff here," Dylan said grabbing a 35mm camera sitting on top of its case atop a console table. "Look at this."

"Take it."

"I intend to." Dylan stuffed it into the duffel bag and continued to look around like a child in a candy store. He saw money crumpled up next to a book and shoved it into his pocket. On the mantle sat an expensive-looking clock that Dylan grabbed to put inside the duffel bag but it slipped from his hand and fell to the floor. When Dylan picked it up, he noticed the face was cracked. He placed it back on the mantle, turning it so it faced exactly as before.

Justin, looking for a specific item, went through the house to find the bedroom where his experience proved most guns were kept.

"What are we looking for?" Dylan asked, following Justin, grabbing things at random.

"An Uzi," Justin answered, opening the closet of a second-floor bedroom at the top of the stairs.

"An Uzi? Damn. Where's a bathroom in this fucking place? I gotta take a piss."

"Yeah, Phoenix told me that about you." Justin joked.

"Yeah, well, I could tell you a few things about her."

"Don't be crass."

"Crass. Fuck you. You don't be an asshole, laughing behind my back. I gotta take a piss, so fucking what?"

"Okay, Dylan. We weren't laughing behind your back. She told me that about you, but we didn't make a big joke about it."

"Whatever, Justin, it's just—ya know—you don't know every-fucking-thing, dude."

Justin stopped what he was doing. "Do we have a problem, here?"

Dylan knew he still needed Justin on his side. He and Phoenix's relationship was doing well but Justin could still sabotage it if he wanted to, plant little seeds, whisper little pretentious words. "No, man, we're cool" he said. "Just don't try to make me look bad in front of Phoenix, that's all."

"That ain't my style." Justin walked away

Dylan went to the open closet Justin just left. Inside, he saw a leather biker's jacket hanging next to camelhair overcoat and a Giorgio Armani suit. He grabbed the leather jacket, thinking it needed to be thrown under a bus to break it in, and put that, too, in his bag. He looked at the suits of navy blue, pin-striped and light gray, at silk ties on the rack that were either solid colors or vertical stripes, and at the shoes of Italian design and oxford-blood wing-tips, off to the side he saw a pair of cowboy boots and Doc Marten's. Dylan grabbed the cowboy boots and shoved them into the bag.

"Found it!" Justin said from a room off the balcony.

When Dylan arrived, he saw Justin, sitting on the floor with his legs crossed, pulling the empty clip from the recently oiled and cleaned Uzi. Justin checked the empty chamber then attempted to put the black metal inside the duffel bag Dylan brought over, but it wouldn't fit. Justin, sitting beside the armoire, looked up at Dylan who begrudgingly removed a few items from the bag.

"Damn, you really found one," he said as Justin handed it to him.

"The Israelis may need it, but this guy doesn't."

Dylan paused a moment to admire the sleek design before placing it in the bag. Suddenly Dylan thought about the story of Red, an old friend in the Four Horsemen, who used his contacts to get a dozen .38s for his fellow members, and Dylan wondered who Justin wanted to kill.

"Is this all you want?"

"Yep."

When they walked upstairs to turned on the light to signal Phoenix they were ready to be picked up, Dylan let Justin take the lead. While walking down the stairs and through the surprisingly small kitchen to the back door, Dylan decided he wouldn't underestimate Justin again.

Phoenix arrived at the back door within minutes after seeing the beacon. She drove up with her lights on and Justin jumped in the front seat, carrying the duffel bag, and Dylan got in back.

"Did you get it?" she asked Justin while pulling out of the driveway.

Justin showed her the unloaded Uzi and smiled.

"That's a disgusting machine," she said with contempt.

"Yeah it is," said Justin earnestly.

"What are you going to do with it?" Dylan asked.

Phoenix and Justin smiled at each other. Justin, in a playful mood, turned to Dylan in the backseat and pointed the gun at him. "Nothing," he said, "unless you fuck with me!"

"Hey!" Dylan spat out. "What the fuck, man!" Dylan moved to the other side of the backseat, not taking his eyes off the black hole in the black barrel. "Son of a bitch!"

"Then it's ack-ack-ack-ack-ack!" Justin continued. Phoenix began laughing.

At first, Dylan couldn't understand why Phoenix was laughing. Thoughts raced through his head and he remembered the gun was unloaded, he had watched Justin unload it, hadn't he? Or did Justin reload as they walked down the stairs? He was about to just grab the barrel and fight it out when he saw Justin smile and put the gun away. When it became apparent there was no danger he tried to compose himself, "Ha-ha-ha!" he started, pulling his hair back. "That's really fucking funny, Justin." But Dylan was thinking: *the bastard made me look like a fool, again, the motherfucker. I just warned him about that shit. I just told him not to make me look bad in front of Phoenix. I just fucking told the son of a bitch!*

Phoenix laughed, "Lighten up, Dylan."

And Dylan, hearing Phoenix tell him to lighten up, knew he'd better or he'd end up losing control of this night and probably Phoenix too.

"You scared the shit out of me!" Dylan said as he forced a smile. "Jesus, I thought you'd gone nuts. Isn't there an asylum somewhere near here?" Justin started laughing and when Dylan heard Phoenix join in, he knew everything was going to be okay. "I think we should check both of you in for evaluation." He looked at Phoenix. "And what are you laughing at, missy? I think I'll keep the present I *waaas* going to give to you."

"A present!" Phoenix dramatically exclaimed. "How sweet. Did you just steal it?"

Dylan leaned up to her and gave her a kiss. "See how you've corrupted me," he said and grabbed her breast.

"Uh-huh." Phoenix said, Dylan's hand still resting on her breast. She could feel her nipple getting hard and wanted to climb into the backseat with him.

Justin turned on the radio. Out of the corner of his eyes, he watched and waited for Phoenix to remove Dylan's hand. The owner of the car had the radio set to a jazz station and Justin, with his heightened periphery, saw Phoenix begin to writhe in the front seat to the sounds of a saxophone and Dylan's touch. *Clearly claiming ownership*, Justin though and changed the station. Top 40 music came on and Justin heard Dylan singing along with Van Halen as he started kissing Phoenix's neck. Justin turned and stared out the window as they left the West End, unable to focus on anything. He reached over without looking and changed the radio station again.

Phoenix dumped the Lincoln on a curb near Justin's Nova, and the three got out. As Justin got into his car, Dylan asked Phoenix if he could talk to her for a minute. Justin started his car and watched Dylan lead Phoenix to a small grove of trees.

In the gray shadows that seemed to embrace the two lovers, Dylan offered Phoenix the black leather jacket he stole from a stranger. "If you're going to ride on the back of my bike, you need a proper jacket," he said, offering Phoenix a ride for the first time. Dylan didn't use his Harley to impress the girls; he didn't use it as a pickup line. When he offered them a ride, it meant a true commitment to him. His women didn't ride *bitch*, they rode *queen*.

"When do you think I can wear it?" she asked, feeling elevated by Dylan's offer.

CHAPTER 17

Inside the Panicosky's garage, sat Dylan's Harley, a clean, customized black chopper with a yellow gas tank. Painted on the tank were the *colors* of the Four Horsemen: four horse's heads split in a mirror image, two facing right and two facing left. One the right, the first horse's head was painted white, looking up, and the second horse's head was red, looking down; facing left was a black horse's head reared up, and the fourth horse, painted green, looked down. Between each pair of heads hung a scimitar. At first, in the dimly lit garage, Phoenix thought the embossed icon was a butterfly.

Inside, the sound of Dylan starting up his bike woke his father out of a dream. When he jumped out of bed and went to the window, he saw his son riding off with a girl in the queen seat. He went back to his empty bed, smiling.

The bike growled under Dylan as he rode under the large harvest moon with Phoenix. Dylan felt Phoenix behind him; her breasts firm against his straight back, her thighs pressing slightly against his hips, her hands gently resting on his legs.

"You've been on the back of a bike before," he said over his shoulder, noticing her casual manner as a passenger. He thought about the women who held on too tight or leaned with him on a turn. "You ride well."

"Thanks. Where are we going?" she yelled above the wind.

Dylan pulled into an unkempt cemetery and rode down the cement path with weeds growing between the cracks. The night silhouetted them against tombstones and graves as Dylan continued to ride to the far end of the graveyard. In the cool and comfortable September night, the stars illuminated clearly where they were: Billy Panicosky's grave.

Dylan turned off his bike and got off without saying a word. He hadn't planned to go there, but now, ten feet away from Billy's weather-beaten mound, he felt it would be disrespectful if he ignored him. He walked to the foot of Billy's grave and stood there, staring out into the dying trees and chipped headstones. Phoenix walked up and stood behind him. Both assumed a moment of quiet respect.

"I love it here," Dylan finally said.

"It's all right." Phoenix had been to graveyards in the middle of the night before.

"This is my brother." Dylan pointed to the limestone marker.

Phoenix stepped closer and read: "William Panicosky." She then read the dates of his birth and death, "What was he... 30?"

"Yeah. He never thought he'd make it to 30."

"Well, he did."

"For a couple of months anyway. How old are you?"

"21."

Dylan nodded. "When Billy was 21, he sat on top of the world. Everybody thought he was immortal, everybody knew him. I'm 25 and I'll never have that."

Phoenix sat down next to Dylan's bike. "You wanna tell me about him, don't ya?"

"Yeah, I guess I do." Dylan sat down next to her, lost in an almost trance-like state, and told her about Billy the Kid. "He taught me how to ride my first bike when I was 6. I lost control of it and ended up riding across my mother's garden, over a wooden fence, and down a ditch, my feet dragging the whole way, trying to stop. It was really weird; it was like I had no idea how to stop. I just kept going, steering like crazy, trying to avoid one thing and running over another. Finally I hit a tree." He stopped to show a small scar by his left eye. "See this? My first scar. Mom was going to kill me for tearing up her garden, but then she saw all the blood that a head wound produces..." He stopped and joined in on Phoenix's laughter.

"Mom started screaming at Billy but he just kinda strolled down, picked up the bike, and said: 'Dylan, the damn brakes are right here.' It was funny somehow and Mom giggled and that was that. My mom calmed down and told Billy to take me upstairs to patch up my wound. 'You broke him,' she joked, 'you fix him. And then both of you come down here to help me fix my garden.'" He paused, reflecting on his brother's sink-or-swim attitude. "He was the Road Captain for his club, the Four Horsemen."

"Really?" Phoenix said, now remembering the emblem on his gas tank. She knew of the Four Horsemen, everybody in the Midwest did, if only by intimation. The club made an impression. People turned their heads to look at them out of curiosity and turned away out of fear—even when only three of its members rode down the highway. They had an untouchable quality about them, a malevolent presence. It didn't seem possible for Dylan to be running with those kinds of men. She looked again at the grave that held such finality for a man Dylan loved and respected. She considered the pale veil that awaits us all and knew that under it is an empty, deteriorating shell of a man who was loved. *And when his tombstone fades away*, Phoenix thought, *who would remember him?*

"What happened?"

"He was alone on a rode trip and got into a fight with some chicken-shit member of some chicken-shit club in Arkansas. We don't know the details. He was shot six times. When the Four Horsemen heard about it, we rode down there—man, what a sight—you ain't seen nothing 'til you see a fucking battalion of the Four Horsemen in formation, wearing their colors, rolling down the highway. Every member was on that ride. They let me ride in his position. It was a great honor." Dylan paused for a moment and Phoenix reached over for his hand. "Anyway, we went down there to TCB. Every fucking club in the country knew about the war—some even joined us—doing recon—but the yellow bastards must've been hiding in some goddamn fuckin' hole because we couldn't find 'em, nobody could. Finally, the state patrol and the county pigs, even the FBI, all forced us to leave by following us, harassing us constantly, throwing some of us in jail, confiscating shit. Finally, we all just rode back. But to this day those cowards don't show their colors."

CHAPTER 18

The dance in the West End affected Justin more than he expected. After Phoenix and Dylan left, Justin stayed downtown and walked the empty streets to find solace in the arms of night. Whenever Justin Sunder felt ill at ease, anxious, nervous, or confused he'd walk under the moon to clear his mind. After the dance, negative memories of his past kept imposing themselves, attempting to take root. Justin refused them but he still felt their effects. After years of walking in shadows, he was finally able to defend himself against all the negative scenes that played out in his mind: all the ostracized years of his young adult life where he was sent away to school, not invited on vacations, treated like a bastard. He fought against his reduction to an angry, insecure, hateful man whom he didn't like at all. Before the accident, Justin Sunder was a strong man. It surprised him how fast one's confidence could be stripped away. He hated the resentment he carried with him, uglier then any seared skin. That wasn't Justin, and he wanted his pride back, his confidence. After years of an internal struggle against the demon inside, eating away at his Cheyenne soul, he found several ways to expunge the negativity. The struggle within manifested itself in many ways and one of them was thievery, which presented its own problem: Phoenix.

Justin walked past a group of men who stared maliciously at him and made comments he didn't hear. Justin, deep in thought, continued to walk and reflect.

Before the accident, Justin had the kind of confidence Dylan possessed. He used to be cocky, arrogant, and ignorant, like Dylan. After the accident and the irreversible damage caused by the casual surgeon, he lost all that self-empowerment. But the night he approached Phoenix he had it all back: the ignorance that allowed him to assert himself, the arrogance that allowed him to approach her, the cockiness that put his leg between hers. He forgot about his scar completely. Everything he thought about himself was positive. He didn't see his scar in the eyes of Phoenix. When he kissed her, he just knew he wasn't going to be turned down. Holding her, he felt beautiful again. And when she turned away, he cursed himself for being so presumptuous. But Justin realized, many years ago, if he continued to be self-conscious about his scar, it would grow to a point beyond his control. Even though Phoenix's rejection hurt, he had learned to master the pain. If he hadn't, he would have become ugly, using the scar as his excuse and his bane. He refused to let that happen and walked straight into the melee of mockery, insult and criticism that awaited him. He refused to be broken by his equestrian peers of his pre-scar days or any one of the people he met after his disfigurement. He refused to be beaten. In some ways his mark wasn't any worse than a young man he met who had severe acne as a teenager that left his entire face scarred with pockmarks. He'd met an adult woman whose limbs never developed as a direct result of a pharmaceutical drug, Thalidomide; a young woman with a glass eye because of a childhood toy of two glass balls attached to a string shattered as she played and sent tiny shards into her eye; a man who had his entire back burned when his Ford Pinto exploded in a rear-end collision; people with scars from knife wounds, gunshots and disease; underdeveloped and overdeveloped limbs; amputees; the list of mental, psychological, and physical draftees continued in an ever increasing fraternity of fractures. He saw people who consciously drew attention to their battle wounds, as if to demand acknowledgment of their handicap. He met others who didn't consider themselves marred in any way, and it bothered Justin that they tried to ignore its presence. He wanted a combination of the two. He wanted honesty without false impressions and humility without insecurity.

As he turned down Market Street, cutting through the small block park, he passed a man in a wheelchair who asked him for spare change.

"Can't help you," Justin said without looking at him. His thoughts continued, uninterrupted.

The friends he made in the night boasted of having open minds, and although he saw those minds close many times, it still allowed them to be less judgmental; unlike the rich he knew who clung together regardless of their offensive personalities. The avaricious people of his past were motivated in developing relationships from fear of offending someone who could help them later. Their friendships, based on superficiality, had a sadly dehumanizing effect: they didn't *talk*, they *interfaced*, they didn't *meet*, they *networked*; they formed mergers and unions. Their clubs were more frightening than any gang he ever saw, and their colors just as uniform.

A car passed him and a voice yelled: "White boy!" but the car didn't stop. Justin walked on, unaffected.

His journey to self-empowerment schooled him in many ways. It taught him how to fight because he allowed his anger to surface much too often. One winter skiing in Taos, New Mexico, he got into a fight where he broke his nose. By an ironic twist of cosmetic justice, his nose healed perfectly and he even lost the slight bump he had on the bridge. After that bit of luck, he resolved to fight only when it was absolutely necessary to defend himself. That decision taught him humility because he walked away from the taunts and jeers he used to run to. He learned to simply wave insults off, not with a sense of humor or with a witty comment, but with resolve. He heard the words but gave them no meaning. The friends he made on his journey taught him loyalty and honesty. The friends he lost taught him sincerity by their lack of it, punctuating its absence and making it larger, clearer, and more real than they intended. By the time Phoenix met Justin, he was strong and confident.

Passing a group of men, one called out to Justin: "Hey, give me a cigarette!"

"Can't help you," Justin said and kept walking.

But now, Justin thought, *but now.... I don't want to dance anymore this dance. And I'm backsliding. I'm losing control again. I wasn't happy here, but where else did I have to go? And then after meeting Phoenix, where could I go?* The impression of his uncle Sitting Wolf appeared in his mind and he held it for several minutes, recalling the few times they actually met. *I could do that. But would she go with me? Now?* The image of Phoenix and Dylan in the car earlier popped into his inner vision. *And what about that? Our relationship will never be that. She'll never love me like I love her.* The idea of Phoenix loving him floated for a moment and then disappeared, leaving a complete void of any thought at all. In meditation, it's called quieting the chattering monkey. Justin walked in peace for several blocks.

Then, as clear as the night sky above him, Justin elucidated what needed to be done. Suddenly his mind unloaded the problem that weighed down his body. Justin, finally making the decision he'd been thinking about for months, turned to go back to his car. The thought of not stealing anymore, made him feel strong, confident, and in control again. As he walked back, he felt lighter than before. He looked up at the night sky, the moon, the stars, and thanked them and his uncle.

CHAPTER 19

"So you belong to a motorcycle gang?" Phoenix asked Dylan, finding it both exciting and worrisome.

"No, not any more. I still have the mark on my tank, but I'm not allowed to wear their colors on my jacket," Dylan said, thinking about the circumstances that led to his decision to quit.

At a dark party one night, a fellow member, Blackjack, whom Dylan never really liked or trusted before even though he was supposed to be a brother, came on to his girlfriend and Dylan exploded. He shoved a knife into Blackjack's gut, sending him to the hospital. Unknown to Dylan, Blackjack wasn't trying to pick up his girlfriend; he was just innocently talking to her, but Dylan felt they were getting too friendly. When Blackjack kissed her on the cheek before he left, Dylan jumped on him. That night Billy told Dylan of his plans to leave the Four Horsemen and suggested Dylan do the same.

"Billy was even getting ready to split," Dylan said. "He was going to move to California and open up a shop there." Dylan stood up and took off his leather jacket. "Anyway, I didn't bring you here to talk about my brother. I just think this is a cool place and he happens to be here."

"Yeah, right."

"I don't care anymore about all that shit. I only care about riding. I'd rather be here than not be able to ride anymore."

Phoenix sat on Dylan's bike. "It's a beautiful scooter."

Dylan walked to her. "There's something about riding a motorcycle. I don't know what it is, but it makes you... I don't know, dream, I guess.

I can't put it into words, but it's just as real. It's like being a part of it all and not just driving through it."

"It's having something big and powerful between your legs," Phoenix said. "That's what it is."

Dylan smiled and took of his shirt. Phoenix looked at his round shoulders, and his smooth, hairless chest. She reached out and touched him, resting her fingers on his dark nipples.

"The last time I was in a junkyard like this," Phoenix said as she squeezed his nipple. "I was saying goodbye to my stinking whore, pimp-bitch mother."

"Don't talk that way about your mother."

"Don't tell me how to talk about anybody." Phoenix pulled her hand away.

"She's your mother."

"What the fuck is that? What does that mean? Just because she gave birth to me, I owe her something? I don't owe her shit! You don't know what you're talking about!"

"All right, baby, you're right. I don't know." Dylan held her hand. They stood together in the dead night, silent for a long time.

Finally, Phoenix slipped her leather jacket off. "You know what I want to do right now?" Phoenix asked, sliding off his bike.

"What?"

"Fuck you, right here." She kissed him, walked over to William's grave, and pulled her shirt off. It fell like a leaf onto Billy's sunken grave. The moon lit upon her body, naked from the waist up. She looked golden in the night. Phoenix spread her legs and put her palm on her thigh.

"Come here," Dylan Panicosky said seriously.

Phoenix moved her hand across her tight stomach, pausing for a moment on the silver in her navel. Her other hand moved up between her lithe breasts to her soft shoulder, then to her neck. She touched her face and pushed the hair out of her eyes.

"I'm not fucking you there."

Phoenix smiled and sank to her knees.

"Get off!" Dylan demanded and stormed over to her, reaching her in three steps. He grabbed the back of her hair and lifted her up. Phoenix grabbed his hand and dug her nails into it. She kicked at him but Dylan wrapped his arms around her torso and picked her up; her foot swung out harmlessly into the night air. He carefully sidestepped his brother's grave as he forced her onto his shoulder and carried her back to his bike. Phoenix, biting and punching, scratching and kicking, left cuts and bruises in Dylan before he dropped her and stepped away. When Phoenix hit the dirt, she pulled out her butterfly knife from her back pocket and quickly opened it while standing up. Flipping her wrist down, turning her hand over, flipping her wrist up—the three movements started and finished in an instant—click-click-click—and the knife blade shot out from the handle. The black blade didn't shine at all in the night, and Dylan, seeing her hand move and hearing sounds he couldn't recognize, had no idea Phoenix now held a knife.

When she took a step toward him and moved her hand slightly out from behind her back, Dylan realized what the sounds were. He smiled, staring at Phoenix. "What are you going to do with that?"

The fury in her stance looked like she'd gone insane. Her hair was disheveled and her light brown skin was slightly darker from the dirt. To Dylan, she looked like a fallen angel. She was out of breath but she had more energy than Dylan knew. But as she walked toward Dylan, her anger dissolved. When she reached him, she smiled and put the knife up to his throat. "You ever do that again and I'll cut your fucking head off."

Dylan pushed his throat onto her blade. "Did I hurt you?"

"You wish."

Dylan smiled. "You pulled out that knife, you wanna use it?" Dylan touched his heart. "Right here."

Phoenix closed the knife and kissed him.

"Cut me, right here," he said, pointing to his chest, his body and mind alert from an almost narcotic rush.

Phoenix parted her lips and exhaled. She opened the knife, tilted her head, and looked up at Dylan. Blood flooding through her body made her skin warm to the touch, she became aware of her sex swelling. She smiled and cut quickly across his chest. The sharp blade painlessly cut a four-inch mark. They watched the trickle of blood flow a bending line, its course plotted by following the contours of his chest muscles, down to the middle of his stomach where it changed course again, following the grooves cut by his stomach muscles.

Phoenix noticed a scar on his bent arm that softly touched her face. The scar had healed well but she could tell it was from a deep cut. She wondered how this new one, which she accidentally cut a little too deep, would heal.

When the thin, dark line flowed into his pants, he took them off and stood there naked. The blood stopped at Dylan's coarse hair. Phoenix wiped her hand across his torso and started caressing his sex with her bloodstained hand. Dylan took her knife and placed it just above the nipple of the breast he cupped in his hand. She took a deep breath and nodded. Dylan made a quick, shallow cut across the left side of her chest. Phoenix squeezed. He dropped the knife. They embraced and kissed, mingling their blood and sweat and sex, mocking the dead in the barren graveyard.

CHAPTER 20

John Bowman's bar had grown exponentially in popularity over the past year. Six months ago he hired another bartender, Jeanette, who John thought was pretty but looked odd in the over-sized men's clothing she wore; she often sported articles of clothing John's father wore in the '40s. Once, when he found an old derby of his father's, he gave it to her as a gift. Jeanette displayed such enthusiasm over the felt pot hat that whenever John came across anything old, he would bring it in for her. To card the college students that hung out in his bar on the weekends, he hired a pleasant, gregarious doorman, Danny-boy, who—in John's opinion—acted queer sometimes, but he'd never seen a man Danny-boy couldn't throw out. He hired Ginny to cocktail occasionally and she always brought new music in for him to play between his sets of oldies. When it was slow, John would teach her how to make drinks. John didn't think Ginny was very attractive but every man through the door tried to pick her up. John didn't know how or when his clientele changed, but they had a good attitude, and they liked his bar and his music, so he didn't think much about it. He let them do what they wanted and rarely did his customers annoy him. Fights only happened once in a blue moon.

Inside, the music and the din of the conversation were so loud Jeanette had to lean across the bar to hear customers order. John, wearing a Hulk T-shirt, made drinks for Ginny who then carried her tray high above her head through the crowd to the patrons in the booths. Danny-boy, wearing a top hat and tails, stood at the door, refusing entrance to two underage girls, which upset their boyfriends who gesticulated wildly before Danny-boy's calm continence. Tapping the toes of his steel-tipped boots, he told them all to leave.

In the back, Phoenix and Bernard played a game of pool, the chalkboard on the wall full of names under theirs. But Phoenix, in good humor, took her time setting up shots and talked with her friend. She danced around the table, dodging people who came and went. Bernard, less talented in avoiding the crowd that pushed in on him and not as animated, leaned against the wall and waited his turn. When Phoenix started to look at a difficult rebound shot, he bet her twenty bucks she wouldn't make it.

"You're on, sailor."

She slowly and deliberately chalked her tip, bent down to bumper level to eye up the shot, checked the straightness of her stick, and with feigned concentration and a little bit of theatrics she bent over again to take the shot. A few moments later Bernard handed her a twenty.

"You want to bet on the next one?" Phoenix asked and winked.

"Shit, bitch, you're fucking me sideways," he said while performing a perfunctory chalking of his cue. "What the hell happened to you?"

"Whatever do you mean?" Phoenix asked with more theatrics than she intended.

"Whatever do you mean?" Bernard mimicked and danced around her. "Who are you, Scarlett O'Hara now? You're acting like a schoolgirl."

"Honey, I was never a schoolgirl."

"So what gives?"

"Dylan Panicosky is what gives; man, I tell you, the boy slays me."

Dylan Panicosky? Bernard thought while staring at Phoenix. *This is gonna kill Justin.* "That's it? Some fucking breeder? Phoenix, what the fuck? Does Justin know?"

"Of course he knows. We all went on a dance together a couple of weeks ago and won forty large."

"And you just made me pay you $20?"

Phoenix did a little curtsy. "And we thank you. Bitch."

Suddenly Bernard's eyes widened. It took a moment before he became fully cognizant of the fatal problem that had unexpectedly arose. Bernard cautiously approached Phoenix who was setting up another shot. He knew what she meant by *dancing*, but he also knew something she didn't. He knew their mark, David. He'd known him for years; he knew what he was like in his most generous moods, but, more importantly, he knew what he did in his most noxious. He also knew about the search going on for information concerning David's lost money. Bernard was a part of that pernicious team.

"I want the motherfuckers found!" David had screamed at his friends in his loft almost two weeks after the dance. "I'm Al Capone in this fucking town; nobody rips me off!"

"It must have happened this weekend," said Brett, a tall, thin man with a blond crew cut.

"What about that nigger? She was acting kinda weird toward the end of the night," said Tony, the newest member of David's circle.

"Yeah, she even left early," Kevin added, winking at Sandy.

"In a hurry, too," Sandy said and smiled, thinking about the girl she and Kevin raped.

"That's because Kevin pumped her so full of horse," Bernard started.

"My horse!" Kevin interrupted and laughed.

"That she freaked out," Bernard continued. "She was practically naked when she left. Where do you think she hid it?"

"Up her ass. Those bitches have big asses."

"And she liked it that way, too, let me tell you."

"Shit, Kevin, she didn't even know you were doing it to her," Bernard said with disdain.

"So what," Sandy and Kevin said at the same time and laughed.

"Stop the fucking clowning!" David jumped in. "Are you fucking kidding me? I'll fuck every one of you up the fucking ass if you don't find the motherfuckers that ripped me off! You don't think I'm serious?"

He grabbed Tony, the closest to him, by the neck and forced him to the floor. Once pinned, David began to rip off Tony's clothes. He tried to fight back but David, fueled with sudden rage, almost broke Tony's arm. David's meaty hand clutched Tony's neck while the other hand pulled down Tony's pants. Tony cried out from the maelstrom in a disembodied voice, but no one intervened. Except for Kevin, who stroked his goatee, everybody sat there motionless watching each other without turning their heads, then looking at Tony, then something on the wall. Nobody made eye contact with David who had his own pants down to his knees. Tony twisted and turned and tried to crawl away, but David had his full weight on top of him. Tony's arms were bent behind his back as David pushed his muscular legs between Tony's who could move little to avoid the rape. Tony felt David's hard cock against his ass and screamed. Suddenly, David stopped. His face changed from a distorted mask to his normal features. Kevin stopped stroking his goatee. Tony escaped to the corner and put his clothes back on. Now, nobody made eye contact with Tony. David's paroxysm possessed him for a moment, but he was now back in control. He pulled his pants up and went over to Tony, apologizing. David hugged him, gave him a kiss on the cheek, and then handed him a gram of heroin. But the message was clear. Bernard was the first to leave.

"Where was this dance?" Bernard asked just below the din at J.B.'s hoping she wouldn't say—

"Downtown, the loft district."

In an instant, Bernard saw the walls fall. The noise of the bar seemed to settle down to a whisper, and he thought everyone heard. He looked around the bar for anybody who might be remotely connected to David. He imagined someone at the bar reading Phoenix's lips, someone coming out of the bathroom hearing just enough to give David a lead. He wished she'd never told him. Phoenix and Justin wouldn't brag about it, that Bernard knew. The only thing he could do was convince them to return the money. When he looked to the front of the bar, he saw Dylan coming in. And Bernard hated him.

"Your bump is here," he said, throwing his cue on the table, scattering the balls.

Phoenix smiled when she saw Dylan walk past Danny-boy with a nod. "And what a bump," she said as she set her stick next to Bernard's.

"Was he with you?"

"Of course," Phoenix said. "I'll be right back." Phoenix gave him a kiss and walked away.

Bernard watched as the crowd seemed to actually part for the two lovers.

CHAPTER 21

The North Star was more brilliant and luminous than ever before and Justin called out to her in a playful mood: "Hey star, come down! I wish to dance with you." *Justin Star Dancer*, he called himself. When Justin walked under a tree that seemed to rise and meet the star, he climbed up the healthy tree that was just starting to lose its leaves. Justin reached as high as he could and sat propped between two branches. *Justin Two Branches*, he announced. He smoked a cigarette and blew the smoke into the sky to give the star a tail. Suspended in the tree, surrounded by early autumn leaves, strong branches and near to the open sky, Justin thought he heard the chanting of his maternal people. As Justin listened, images of a great cloud-wreathed northern mountain, a strong, green, and fertile land, and a beautiful butte passed before him. At the end, the first thing Justin focused on was a singular leaf falling from the tree he sat in. *Justin Falling Leaf*, he proclaimed.

As he walked up the alley back home, he had a feeling of inner peace. He decided to tell Phoenix of his decision to stop stealing. After winter, he thought, in the spring, he would leave to visit his uncle; and he would ask Phoenix to join him. When he caught movement in Phoenix's bedroom window, he looked up and saw her and Dylan. They stood together, close, holding each other in a tender embrace. The candles, glowing red in the background, outlined the two forms coming together. He watched them, merging into one, feeling like a voyeur, but unable to pull his eyes away from the amorous image framed by the window. The two figures in love undressed each other and then moved away.

Justin stopped in the alley next to a dumpster. He couldn't go home now. He couldn't bare listening to the ecstasy coming from Phoenix's bedroom. He imagined Phoenix in bed with Dylan; the candles burning, throwing shadows on the wall of the two naked lovers. The white curtains blowing in the wind complementing the movements of Phoenix. Her hand squeezing the white bed sheets as she approached an orgasm from the oral talents of her lover. Her soft, round, golden mound, glistening like it did the first time he saw Phoenix naked while skinny-dipping with some friends. The guttural noises, the passionate sounds of two bodies coming together... He stopped himself from thinking about them anymore. He turned and walked away, but like a photograph, the image of Phoenix in the window served as a catalyst to memories. He looked back and half hoped—half expected—to catch a glimpse of Phoenix in the window, alone, looking out into the ally. The white crescent moon in the cloudy sky and the calm, quiet night reminded him of the first time they danced together.

The first time he realized he loved her was on a night similar to this one. He was waiting outside and saw Phoenix in the window. Her shadowed frame profiled through the window like an image untouchable. Then, just a flash of her eyes, like glowing emeralds, and she was gone.

It was that memory he carried in his mind as he walked. Phoenix in silhouette, not real, three-dimensional or tangible, not flesh and bone. The echo of Phoenix was all he wanted now for the real Phoenix was being touched by another man. And Justin once again thought about his future with Phoenix and wondered if what he witnessed was a sign, a message, if it was real or an illusion.

On a dark passage of the street lined with trees came a voice that Justin at first ignored.

"Excuse me. Excuse me. Pardon me, sir?"

There was a desperation in the voice that halted Justin.

"Yes?" He said looking at the man he thought was drunk or high on something. For a moment he hoped for a fight.

"Is the Arch-way that way?" The man pointed east, his large, round head bobbing a little.

"No, the *Arch*," Justin corrected him, "is that way." He pointed north.

"Will the bus take me there?"

Justin looked into his oblique, slant eyes, one of them slightly crossed. It took him a moment to focus on the eye that looked directly at him. He looked at his flat nose, his small ears, and thought: *Down's.* "It all depends on which bus you take," he offered.

"So I should get on the other road going that way?"

"Yes," Justin said, tempted to leave him.

"I can ask the bus driver, I guess, huh?"

"Are you sure they're still running this late?"

"They said they did."

"What's your name?"

"Darren."

"Darren, come with me." Justin said and walked away. Darren followed.

"What's your name?"

"Justin."

"Justin, does your face hurt?" Darren asked innocently referring to Justin's scar.

Justin laughed. "Sometimes, Darren, sometimes it hurts a great deal."

"I'm sorry."

The two walked to J.B.'s and Darren told Justin his story of how he became lost. How some kids had scared him when he asked them for directions, and how they demanded money for their information. How he tried to hitchhike but not even a cab would pick him up. He was going to walk all the way to the Arch because he knew his hotel was near it. "If I can just find the Archway," he said, "I could get home. So I started walking."

If Justin hadn't come along, Darren would have walked all night and still not have found the Archway. When they reached J.B.'s, Justin gave him $20 as he passed the bouncer sitting at the door.

"Hey Danny-boy"

"Justin. Is your friend old enough?"

"He's just gonna wait for a cab, okay?"

Danny-boy looked at Darren. "No problem. Have a seat," he said to Darren, pointing to the barstool next to him. "You can help me card the pretty girls."

Justin turned to Darren. "I'm gonna go call a cab for you. When it pulls up front, they're gonna honk their horn, so listen for it. You'll have to go out to them, they won't come in and get you, okay? After you get in the cab, tell the driver the name of your hotel and that he should take Broadway. Don't let him take any side roads, okay?"

"Okay. Thank you, Justin."

Justin left Darren and approached the end of the bar where John and Ginny were arguing over what music to play next while a half-dozen patrons patiently waited for their drink orders. In the end, Ginny got her way and The Cure was soon heard over the speakers. Ginny turned it up before pointing to a young man's empty pint glass. When he nodded, Ginny grabbed his glass and pulled another draft. Justin watched Ginny and John behind the bar, taking orders, side-stepping each other, conducting their orchestra with their clients half the time simply by pointing at the customer and waiting for their nod. Patrons felt honored when one of them actually stopped for a moment on a busy night and talked to them.

"What's your poison tonight, Justin?"

"You freezing your vodka yet?"

"What? No. What bar freezes their vodka?" John asked and wiped down the bar in front of him. "I've got ice and I've got vodka, that's about as frozen as it's gonna get."

"Then I'll take your ice and some of your Stoli's. In a frozen mug."

"Now, you know we don't do that either."

"Thank God—or Wonder Woman," Justin said referring to John's t-shirt. "Also, a Pepsi for my friend at the door."

John looked toward the front of the bar. "He doesn't drink Pepsi."

"Not Danny-boy, the guy sitting with him."

"Friend of yours?"

"Just met him. Lost. *Lost soul.* Helping him find his way home."

"Does he want his drink in a frozen mug with ice?"

Justin smiled for the first time that night and looked over at Darren carding two pretty girls. Justin was glad he ran into Darren when he did—it helped him forget about Phoenix for a while.

John left and Ginny dropped a shot of tequila in front of him. "I don't do tequila," she said. "Where's Phoenix?"

CHAPTER 22

Justin watched all the couples in J.B.'s and felt buried alive in the cramped coffin of St. Louis, suffocating in the absence of Phoenix's love. On his way out the door, he skillfully walked through the crowd, anticipating a drunk's hand gesture, taking a quick step, following someone who made a hole, and moving his shoulders to avoid colliding into someone.

"Whoa, Justin!" Bernard called out. "You gonna walk right past me and not say hello?"

Justin made a detour and moved to Bernard who made room next to him at the bar. "You've got to slow down," Bernard continued. "You gotta take it easy, you know? Take time and smell the barley and the hops, and here, look at this, stale pretzels! You've gotta stay and help me enjoy all this."

Justin laughed. Bernard was high on something. "He's closing soon, I think," Justin said.

"He should be closed *down* soon. He should be closed down and have his liquor license taken away from him, he should—" Bernard stopped and saw John standing behind him. "Hi, John!" He waved and smiled.

"Watch it there, Bernie," John said in good humor and walked away.

Bernard turned to Justin, "Okay, here it is, let's go to the east side. Come on, let's cross the big drink, old man river, the mile-wide Miss'sip! I'll keep all the queens away and buy some poppers."

Justin smiled at his dear friend. "Don't beg, Bernie." Justin said and pinched Bernard's cheek. "Yeah, okay, I've got a few bucks, let's go."

"Yeah, a few bucks, I know," Bernard said like a disappointed father confronting his child who just lied to him.

"How do you know?"

"Phoenix told me. Come on, let's go."

"She did? When did you see her?"

"Here, earlier tonight."

"Dylan was invited to the dance. Think it might've been a mistake," Justin offered.

"That ain't the half of it, brother."

"She's with him now."

"I know."

"How do you know?"

Bernard didn't answer. He wanted to talk about the dance at David's. "Come on."

In Bernard's car Justin looked through his collection of tapes, reading the titles and the artists: Dead Or Alive, Frankie Goes To Hollywood, Culture Club, and throwing them over his shoulder into the back seat.

"You picking those up later, or what?"

"What?"

"Nothing, never mind, please continue," Bernard said throwing a couple of tapes in the back seat himself.

"Don't you have any decent music?" Justin finally asked, and Bernard reached down and grabbed a tape at random.

"This is the best band in the world," he said, not looking at the tape he put in. The humming sound of the heads being cleaned came over the speakers.

"Oh, yeah, I've heard this band."

Bernard turned down the volume, and the two drove in silence for a while.

After sitting in Bernard's uncharacteristically quiet car for several miles, Justine finally asked: "What?"

"The loft job was very uncool, Justin," he finally said. "I know this guy. He's not somebody you wanna fuck with."

"You know him?"

"His name is David."

"We know."

"Yeah, well, one thing you don't know is that he's a mean, manipulative, conniving, dangerous son of a bitch!"

"You're right. We didn't know that!"

"Justin, the guy did snuff films in L.A."

"Fuck it, I ain't in L.A."

"You don't have to be."

"So, he's demented. We'll be cool."

"Let me tell you a story, okay?"

"Please."

"When he was 20 he got stoned one night, I mean really stoned—I forgot all the drugs he said he was on—which, by the way, he told me not as an excuse for what I'm about to tell you he did, but rather as a casual list," Bernard stopped for a second then continued. "Anyway, he's stoned, right? And he comes across a women in the middle of the night and rapes her." Bernard paused again. "It was his mother."

"Jesus Christ!"

"Can you imagine being raped by your own son? Can you imagine what must have been going through her mind?"

Justin imagined for a second and shook his head as if to remove the image from his mind before it set too firmly.

"As repulsive as that is," Bernard continued, "David didn't really know he was raping his mother. Now, a normal man would go insane once he found out what he did, right? Not David. David didn't feel anything, I mean nothing. I know, I've talked to him. He blames her for looking too sexy, for being at the wrong place at the wrong time, karma, fate, for not fighting back hard enough, for not telling him who she was—forget the fact that he broke her jaw when she let out her first scream and practically knocked her unconscious—for maybe her really wanting it and liking it—"

"—Wow."

"Wow is right. His mother was the one who went insane, and when she attacked him one night with a butcher knife, his father tried to intervene and he was the one who got stabbed in the throat. David cursed him for being so stupid as to walk into the blade. At the trial, his insane mother pointed at the rapist that she no longer saw as her son but David was never even questioned. The death of his father was found to be accidental, and his insane mother was put away. David left the country for a while. Now he's back and he's set up here in St. Louis."

"Wow. And this guy is a friend of yours?" Justin asked incredulously.

"No, of course not, not after I heard all his stories, of course not, no, but now it's too late. I avoid him when I can, but when he calls I answer. Would you want somebody like that as your enemy?"

"No."

"Well, you do now. Return the money. Use all your skills and break in to put the money back It'll feed his ego. I can see him now, strutting around, 'I'm Al Capone in this fucking town! Nobody rips me off—and if they do, when they find out it was me, they put the shit back!' He'll love it, Justin. He'll still want you found, but he won't look as hard. Put it back, please.

CHAPTER 23

Inside the bar on the east side, the music pounded out an insistent beat like a pheromone. The air smelled of musk, cigarettes, perfume, and sweat. At the far end of the bar a leather dyke arm-wrestled with a drag queen who just finished performing upstairs. Bernard and Justin stood next to them and ordered their drinks, then moved to the edge of the dance floor. The men and women, rutting on the dance floor, were lost in their own worlds with little concern of what went on around them.

Justin watched the parade in front of him. When a Marlboro man walked by, darting his tongue in and out under his bushy mustache at Justin, Bernard flicked his cigarette at him.

"So, Justin, tell me what's buggin' you. Tell me about you, Phoenix, and Dylan. I know you want to, so stop looking silly by trying to evade the issue. Spill your guts all over the place, all over the floor. Let the porters clean it up in the morning. Rip out your heart. Put it on your sleeve for all to see. Cry on my strong, tattooed shoulders. Come on, Justin dearest!"

Justin looked at him. "My, how you do go on."

"Yes, I know."

Finally, Justin said to Bernard, "You know what bothers me most about all this? I've done such a good job convincing her we're just friends, because that's what she wanted, and now it's too late to do anything about it. I lied to her about my feelings so she wouldn't be disappointed in me, and now I'm the one miserable. I used to think we had something special between us, something united by a beautiful twisted cord that only we shared; but now I realize the folly in my lie... my life. I can't continue this any longer, Bernard. I now know the different faces her love wears, and it's not going to change for me. And it hurts."

Bernard lowered his eyes. "Yes, it does, Justin." Bernard had seen the different faces of Justin's love. As Phoenix was unable to return Justin's love, Justin was unable to return Bernard's. But, whereas Bernard was able to accept the limitations of their homosocial relationship, Justin could not accept the limitations of his and Phoenix's heterosexual relationship. He understood that love couldn't be controlled by a dart, as they are often misaimed.

Bernard looked up into Justin's eyes, but before he could say anything, a young blond boy interrupted them with no shirt on and a nail pierced through each nipple, his hair, long and stringy.

"Joey wants to buy you a drink," he said to Justin handing him a beer.

Justin smiled, "I just bought one, thanks."

The boy set the beer down next to Justin's. "If you don't take this, Joey will be hurt."

Bernard interjected, "Tell Joey he doesn't want the drink."

"If you don't take it Joey will kick my ass." He laughed uncomfortably.

Justin accepted the drink. "Okay, where is he? I want to thank him."

He pointed to a tall brunette standing across the dance floor. She was dark and sensual. Her breasts pressed firmly against the fabric of her low-cut dress, her shapely legs accentuated by her heels. Although she wore more makeup than Justin liked, she was still attractive.

The boy walked off and Bernard and Justin's conversation ended. Justin walked across the dance floor to thank her, and Bernard followed. But before they reached her, someone called out Bernard's name. Justin turned to see who it was.

"David, how ya doing, man?" Bernard said as a way of introducing Justin to his new nemesis.

"Fine, Bernard, what's up?"

"Oh, you know, David, just enjoying the decadence of it all."

David took a step closer and looked at him. "If I can help, Bernard, let me know."

"I will, David, I will," Bernard said repeating the name, trying to avoid an introduction. He looked over at Kevin, who stood behind David, and nodded. He hoped Justin would walk away. Bernard had seen David's soul-piercing look on meeting people. It was uncanny how David could pick things up, almost supernatural.

What Bernard thought was subtle, the big man standing too close read as obvious. David learned early in life how to read people and assess them quickly and effectively. He had to know immediately what kind of people he was dealing with. David, a big man who never slouched, even when talking to someone two heads shorter than himself, used his size and his many developed talents to help him learn what wasn't being told verbally. He sometimes stood close as if even the scent of the person would help him formulate an opinion on their character. A nervous quiver—in the hands or lips—could be caused by excitement, fear, or anger. If it was fear, then David would relax and be on the offense, but if it was anger, their adrenaline was pumping and David had to be alert and on the defense. David would shake hands and hold it as if their vibration could reveal something. He would stare into their eyes, looking for meaning pooled in the size of their pupils and where they looked, and where they didn't look; did they avoid eye contact or hold it almost aggressively? He observed the movement of their eyes, if they darted to the right when asked a question they were trying to recall, and the answer was probably the truth, but if they darted to the left, even slightly, they were probably lying. What he read in Bernard's odd behavior was panic. *Why is Bernard nervous?* With his missing $40,000 on his mind, David's senses were dangerously heightened. He turned his back on Bernard and fixed his eyes on his companion. "Evening," he said to Justin.

Justin stood face to face with David and smiled. "How are you?" Justin said matching David's seemingly casual observance. He noticed David didn't make any movement to indicate he wanted to shake hands so Justin kept his down by his side.

"Fine," David said, taking a step closer towards Justin. "How are you?"

Bernard watched them, both confident, both strong, both somehow assessing each other, and for the first time Bernard didn't fear David.

David remembered seeing Justin before and he liked the way he carried himself, the way he handled himself. The man in front of him now, who mirrored him, was the reason for Bernard's reaction earlier. He didn't know why Bernard was so ashamed of being with this guy; he thought he misread Bernard earlier. It wasn't panic he showed but apprehension, maybe embarrassment. He smiled at Justin and asked him his name. They finished their introductions by exchanging a handshake that David initiated. Afterward David excused himself and walked away.

"Do you think he has any cola?" Justin asked Bernard as David walked with the owner to a private room at the other end of the bar.

"What?" Bernard asked, surprised. "For you?"

"For us. Sure, why not?"

"Didn't you see how he looked at you? Didn't you sense the danger in his eyes, the way he surveyed you? Are you blind, Justin?"

"I saw."

"And now you want me to ask him for some coke? Don't you think it'd be a good idea to maybe lay low?"

"No," Justin said with a smile. "I don't."

"What if his money is marked, or something?"

"Bernard..."

"Okay, okay." Bernard shook his head. "I'll ask."

After Bernard walked off Justin looked over to see Joey still waiting for him. As Justin approached, Joey began to smile.

"Thanks for the drink," Justin said.

"You're welcome," Joey said, her voice slightly effeminate but obviously male.

Justin looked again at her silicone chest and smiled. "You make a beautiful woman, Joey."

"Always have," she said, sucking on the straw of her drink. "What's your name?"

"Justin." He thought about telling her he was straight but he anticipated her saying "So am I." He wondered if Joey's penis had been removed.

They shook hands, Joey automatically taking the submissive role. Joey's friend who brought over the drink whispered something into her ear and Justin heard Joey say, "Go away you little twink, go find yourself an auntie." She pulled a small container from her purse and sprayed it into a monogramed handkerchief. The smell of ether permeated the area around them.

Across the bar, David watched Joey and Justin as the manager talked in his ear. He observed Justin waiting patiently as Joey put the cloth inside her mouth and inhaled the fumes. He noticed Bernard walk over to Kevin, and then turned back to watch Joey and Justin.

The first time David met Joey was during a show upstairs when Joey impersonated Madonna. He bought her a few drinks and spent the night with her. Sleeping with a manufactured woman turned him on. He also liked her split personality—one moment waiting on him, straightening his tie, getting him a clean ashtray—and the next moment throwing her full beer bottle at the head of an impersonator who started doing her Madonna on stage.

Through the flashing lights and the moving people, David watched Justin about to take a hit off the handkerchief offered by Joey when suddenly Bernard intervened. *What is he doing?* David watched Bernard's behavior. *Is he jealous of* Joey? *Did Bernard not want to share this interesting, scarred man that carried himself like nobility?* He was anxious to see how Joey would react when Bernard took her man. Bernard removed the handkerchief from Justin's hands and dropped it at Joey's feet. Joey glared at him as he ushered Justin across the dance floor.

"Joseph's having a sex change," Bernard said, approaching a section of the bar draped in heavy, red velvet in a maze-like fashion designed to offer privacy.

"No shit, really? What, am I a troglodyte, Bernard? He's a man with tits. What do you think?" Justin followed Bernard into the labyrinth that had tables, chairs, and settees at varying intervals.

They walked the makeshift corridors lit from pink lights fastened to the floor. When the travelers inside the maze found a spot, they'd put something over the light for additional privacy.

"Joey knows this place like the back of her hairy little hand."

Justin smiled. "I bet, but don't you think his tits looked a lot like Phoenix's?"

"I may be wrong here, but sleeping with Joey just because his tits look like Phoenix's is really sick," Bernard said turning a corner where they found an unoccupied space.

"Bernie, I have no desire to sleep with Joey. Besides, you know if I was ever going to sleep with a man, it'd be you."

"I should be so lucky."

The two sat down on an exhausted sofa. Bernard put half a gram of cocaine in an empty vial and handed the other half to Justin who used the corner of his driver's license to scoop up a bump from the corner of the little brown envelope.

CHAPTER 24

Phoenix watched Dylan sleep. His smooth, rounded eyelids made his face look like a Greek statue. His lips were puckered slightly, as if offering Phoenix a kiss, and his breathing was slow and steady. Phoenix looked at his bronze arm bent over the white sheets, his hand lightly resting on his chest, his thumb next to a clean but convex scar. She looked at her own mark and touched it; hers had healed into a fine clean line. When Dylan turned in his sleep, his leg slid out from under the covers and Phoenix admired his tanned thigh, bent knee, and dark calf. Phoenix put on her kimono, picked up the pillows that had fallen on the floor, and folded up the comforter that had been thrown off the bed. She walked through the apartment, restless, cleaning and straightening, watering the plants. Justin was right. When your body gets used to staying up all night, it's hard to break its rhythm.

She wondered where Justin was; she hadn't seen him all night. *What's he doing?* She remembered the times they were out all night together, alone or with their friends. Dinner, nightclubs, opening nights at galleries, fragments of memories passed through her mind. She smiled and felt, to her amazement, a little jealous that he was out without her. When she saw her saxophone, she thought about playing it. But then suddenly she remembered the renovated old movie palace from the '20s—the Fox Theater—where Justin had taken her several times to see performances and she knew instantly what she wanted to do. She walked into her bedroom and touched Dylan lightly on the face. Immediately his eyes shot open.

"Sorry."

Dylan looked up at her, blinking, trying to focus.

"What's up, honey?"

"I'm bored."

"What do ya wanna do?"

"There's a place on Grand. The Fox. I was thinking about going there."

"What for?"

"I want to play on its stage."

"Phoenix, it's three in the morning."

"I know."

Dylan rolled over. "You go."

"Without you? Yeah, okay. I'll see ya in a couple of hours." Phoenix got dressed and left the room.

After she had all her gear together, she picked up her saxophone and started headed for the door.

"Where we going again?" Dylan asked suddenly appearing out of the bedroom as she passed.

They drove past the baroque terra cotta facade of the Fox Theater twenty minutes later.

Breaking in was a lot easier than Phoenix thought it would be. She and Dylan simply climbed up the iron steps of the fire escape and went through an open window. Inside she walked the elephant-patterned carpet straight to the surprisingly small stage and started playing, disregarding the threat of any security guard or system.

The music, low and lingering, traveled through the large, colorful theater, up its ornate columns, floating in the Siamese-Byzantine temple full of gold leaf, jewels, and brass trim.

Dylan stood next to her for a while, watching her play, but when Phoenix moved down stage, Dylan exited. He didn't know much about theater, but he knew this was Phoenix's solo. He walked behind stage and started reading the autographs written on the corridor walls leading to the green room, but after only recognizing a few, he lost interest and explored elsewhere. He found the huge Wurlitzer organ but didn't know how to switch it on, so he couldn't accompany Phoenix's bluesy music that filled the large, empty theater. He sat on the lap of the ten-foot high

Hindu goddess statue on the side of the stage and lit a cigarette. When he kicked his foot out he accidently broke off a small piece of the statue and decided he'd better go someplace else.

Phoenix's music, suspended in the canopied dome studded with brilliant stones and vibrant colors, dropped slowly onto the plush, red velvet seats. Her soulful music filled the lavish hall with the lone melody of an original composition of Horatius Alastair, dedicated to Phoenix.

While listening to Phoenix, Dylan walked through the theater. He opened the Burmese shrine doors that led to the large lobby. Dylan sat down on one of the four high-backed red velvet throne chairs and swung his leg over an armrest in the form of a camel. The theater and Phoenix's music had a strange affect on Dylan who sat quietly, staring out into the elaborately decorated lobby.

But suddenly the music changed. At first, Dylan thought it was some kind of jazz, but then he recognized the music as angry. He thought about going to her.

An insidious memory of Phoenix's mother, Lucinda, crept into Phoenix as she played. She fought them through her music for a while, but eventually her anger and hatred toward her mother won. The music she offered was like an argument heard from a child. One voice was low, soft, and strong while the other was high, staccato and with no discernible melody. Slowly the tender reverberating voice stopped completely. The instrument opened in her mind a floodgate broken by the notes her deft fingers produced. The hall was filled with the music of dark alleys and deadly drugs and desperate lovers. She played the saxophone with empirical knowledge.

Lucinda decided her teen daughter Phoenix should be introduced into the life of prostitution. Phoenix's mother, a veteran of the New York streets, learned early how she could trade her body as payment for things she wanted. Her first trick acquired for her a bicycle from an older boy up the street.

Lucinda made a profitable living for a while, but at 30 her body already sagged, her face deteriorated and her hair matted. One evening she turned to her young daughter whose father was unknown.

"Phe, honey, I been takin' good care of you all these years, haven't I? Well, I thinks it's time ya start takin' care yourself. I thinks it'll do ya good. It'll teach ya 'sponsibility. When I was your age, I had me apartments and men friends that paid for everything!" She fell into a chair. "Whoa, let me tell ya! Alls I had to do was gives them what they wives couldn't and I was set up! Now, of course, I don't want'cha to be no slut about this but I thinks I could set ya up with the right contacts. Ya know what I mean?" Her mother sat next to the young Phoenix and continued. "What I'm thinking about is a gentleman I knows in Jersey. He's a little weird sometimes, ya know? Sometimes he don't even touch ya." Lucinda held Phoenix's hand. "You could handle that couldn't cha?"

Phoenix looked at her mother. "Yeah, sure."

"That's my baby! Now, you ain't gots to have sex with him the first time. I'll lets him know right up front." She smiled then looked at Phoenix. "Ya have to use whatcha got when ya got it, Phe, 'cause after a while, nobody wants it."

Dylan, in the lobby of the Fox, decided to go to Phoenix. He walked past the elephants and the monkeys decorating the walls, under the grim stone faces, and the golden vultures on top the encircling colonnade, up the staircase flanked by seated lions and strange beasts.

Fourteen-year-old Phoenix went to her room and packed as much as she could—without raising suspicion—into an oversized shoulder bag. She left without looking at her mother. At the door, Lucinda called out, "Don't forget to get paid up front, baby!"

Phoenix walked out the door with no intention of going to Jersey. Six months later, she met Horatius Alastair.

By the time Dylan entered the beautiful golden theater, Phoenix's thoughts had turned back to Horatius and her music changed again. When Dylan saw Phoenix standing alone on the empty wooden stage, he felt a sense of pride and longing. After she finished, Dylan approached her.

"How did you learn to play like that?"

"Juilliard," she said almost to herself.

"Where?"

"I used to live with a man in New York who taught at Juilliard. He taught me," Phoenix said, looking down at her sax.

"I'm sorry, Phoenix, but I don't wanna hear about your ex-lovers."

"He wasn't a lover, Dylan. He was a friend," she said, wondering if he was still alive. "A very dear friend." She recalled the circumstances that caused them to part company.

"I'm sorry, Phoenix, you know I love you like a daughter," he had said over a large breakfast he'd prepared, "but I can't risk my reputation being dragged through the muck and the mire over these unfounded rumors."

Phoenix looked at the abundant food on the table and couldn't find her appetite. She glanced around the apartment at all the familiar objects for the last time. Her throat contracted and tears started to form on the edge of her emerald eyes. "I understand," she said. "When do you want me to leave?"

"I think the sooner, the better." Horatius pushed his full plate away and poured another mimosa for himself and Phoenix. *Her eyes,* he thought, *shimmering for all the wrong reasons.* "I set you up in an apartment a friend of mine has available for a couple of weeks before the new tenants move in." When he saw Phoenix drop her shoulders and slump in the chair, he felt himself dropping, too. "I'm going to give you some money. But then that has to be it. I can't see you again."

CHAPTER 25

The night continued to bring more and more people into the dance club on the east side. It would be light out by the time the bar closed and the 50 remaining patrons, leaving the comfort of their bar, stumbled out into the dawn. Dozens of lovers would have come and gone. The lights of the dance floor would be replaced by the color of the sunrise. Some people would leave to eat breakfast and others would go home. The few who still had the energy would end their night between someone's legs.

Bernard and Justin, high on the coke they kept putting up their noses, danced with Gypsy, a lipstick lesbian, and her lover, who wore horn-rimmed glasses and had her hair in a bun. Carl, who liked to frequent gay clubs because the straight women there were easy to pick up, moved about the club and talked casually to everyone he met. Phillip, his nose and forehead shining from his makeup, walked in with Carl. Ginny, who had just gotten off from J.B.'s, bought shots for her friends and tipped the bartender more than he deserved. Between dances, they all went upstairs to watch the drag show. Joey, who sent Justin another drink, leaned against the bar and watched the girls on stage. She didn't perform in drag anymore since her breast implants and impending sex change disqualified her as an impersonator.

Justin and Bernard left just before the sun rose. The glow that heralded its arrival was the only light in the sky. While walking to Bernard's car, Justin suddenly thought about how he would react once he saw Dylan walking around his apartment, like lovers do, as if he lived there. Suddenly he felt a pain like a twisted, wet knot drying in his gut.

Suddenly the angry voices of men in a car called out, "Faggots!"

"Queers!"

"Hey, let me shove my baseball bat up your ass!"

Laughter from inside the four-door sedan muffled the next volley of insults.

Justin looked around. He and Bernard were the only people out front, and the verbal threats were obviously directed to them.

"Suck my big, fat dick!"

Justin continued to walk. He'd heard insults grunted at him from drunks before.

"Sick bastards! Move back to San Francisco!"

Bernard yelled a mild insult over his shoulders and kept walking. But that was all the four men in the car needed.

The car stopped and four men got out. The driver, anxious to be a part of the mob, forgot to put the car in park and it started to roll away. The others kept walking toward Bernard and Justin while the driver turned his car off. One of them held a baseball bat, jacking off the large phallic symbol and smiling. Justin and Bernard stopped and calmly turned to face the four men. Bernard pulled out his brass knuckles with an attached blade and held it behind his back, waiting for the redneck with the bat.

"Come on faggot!" The man smiled, revealing several chipped teeth.

"I always come on faggots," Bernard said and Justin laughed.

"Fuck you!"

"Oh, please, that's the best your little Cro-Magnon brain can come up with? 'Fuck you'?"

The four men surrounded the two. Bernard had his arms crossed to hide the weapon attached to his fist. Justin's extended peripheral vision allowed him to see all but one, the one behind him. He turned so his friend and he stood back to back. Bernard focused on the one with the baseball bat, but he only saw the bat. Justin inventoried the men who encircled them. The one in front of him had short blond hair and a sparse, scraggly blond beard and mustache. To Justin's right, he saw a cowboy hat. To his left, he saw a white sleeveless shirt and thick arms. They all stood there for a moment in silence. A few people leaving the bar saw the activity down the road and continued to walk on, giving the group of men a wide berth.

Finally, Bernard said, "I'm bored with these simpletons. Come on, Justin, let's go. Have fun with that bat," he said as he started to step out of the circle.

"I will," the chipped toothed man said and started his swing. But Bernard's hand shot out with the strength of metal and hit him in the face, shattering his nose and breaking his cheekbones. The man followed his bat to the cement sidewalk and landed hard, screaming. Both Justin and the driver reached down for the baseball bat at the same time and wrestled for control. Bernard punched the driver in the back and Justin was able to quickly twist the bat free. He hit the driver hard in the gut and the man fell to the ground, spitting up blood beside his fallen cowboy hat. Thick, muscular arms grabbed Bernard, and Justin hit his friend's assailant in the neck, almost breaking it. The strong man collapsed onto the gray concrete as if his strings had been cut. The last young man, naïve and new to this, remembered the handgun tucked in the back of his pants and awkwardly pulled out a 9mm Smith and Wesson. Pointing the pistol at Bernard, feeling the victor, he hesitated for one second. That brief moment of contemplation cost him. Justin turned and cracked the bat across his wrist. Screams came from the mouth surrounded by a boy's beard. The gun fell to the ground and Justin picked it up.

The four mangled men laid there. Bernard grabbed the bat from Justin. He wanted to beat them to death. He held the bat, ready to strike. He wanted to damage them, cripple them. Bernard, like Justin, wondered how many gay men were beaten up by these cowards, how many lesbians were raped as they tried to prove their manhood. Bernard stood there with his bladed brass knuckles and a baseball bat, wanting to kill them. Justin watched. He would allow Bernard a few hits, a few broken bones, but would stop him if he went too far.

Bernard struggled with his own conscious. He wanted to kill them, but he couldn't. *They would have killed me*, he kept saying to himself, staring at the guy with his hand dangling in a poetic dance. *They would have killed us. They would have killed Justin!*" Suddenly Bernard ran over and took out his rage on the car of the crippled men. He beat the dark blue sedan as if he were trying to purge himself. He smashed the tinted windows as if they were their eyes, blinding them forever; the hood, like it was their head; the doors, the body, the trunk, the top—all previously without blemish—became dented. He took the knife attached to his knuckles and slashed their thick tires.

Justin watched but then decided they'd better leave before the police came. The men at Justin's feet were either passed out or crying. He walked over to his friend and gently took the bat away from him. Bernard stopped. He stood there, still, and calm. He looked over at the four men bathed in crimson, their blood pooling around them glowed in the new sun.

"Let's go," Justin said softly and then tapped the car's side view mirror, cracking it.

"Nice touch," Bernard said, taking the bat from Justin and tossing it into the backseat.

They walked past the four men trying to get up, crying out to Bernard and Justin for help.

CHAPTER 26

Justin and Bernard drove in silence until they were ready to talk about the fight. When they did, they talked about the choreography. They were both proud—of themselves and each other. They allowed themselves a little revelry and then got quiet again. Finally Bernard spoke. "I always knew you could kick some ass when you wanted to."

"I had no idea how vicious you could be."

"Only when it's called for, Justin."

"I suppose this was one of those times."

"I'm glad you were with me."

"Maybe if I wasn't here it wouldn't have happened."

"Then it would have happened to somebody else."

"Probably."

"I tell you, Justin, the way you handled yourself back there is why I fell in love with you. You don't overreact, you don't underreact, you're perfect. It's like you're in perfect sync with yourself. I do still love you, you know that don't you?"

"Yes. And I love you too, Bernard." Sometimes Justin wished he could return Bernard's love physically but he couldn't, and Bernard knew that he couldn't. He respected Bernard for his ability to accept the relationship for what it was and not for what it could be, to enjoy the company without pain. He wanted to say something to Bernard, but he didn't know how to begin. He wanted to explain his feelings, but he knew he didn't have to.

When Bernard pulled up to Justin's loft, Justin asked him if he could kiss him good night.

Bernard quickly turned to Justin but he didn't see love, defeat, or even pain in Justin's eyes. What he saw was pity.

"Why?"

"I don't know."

"Don't fuck with me, Justin. Don't tease me. Don't insult me. A kiss? Suddenly now you want to kiss me? Why?"

Justin was silent.

"To prove to yourself you're not a fag?" Bernard asked. "To see if you *are* a fag? To see if maybe you'll like it?"

"No, Bernard."

"Then why?"

"I was just thinking of how my unrequited love for Phoenix is like your unrequited love for me."

"You just now figured that out?"

Justin paused. "Yeah, I guess I just did."

"Well, con-fucking-gratulations!"

Justin turned and stared out the window. *Why did it take me so long to figure that out? How could I be so selfish? So inconsiderate to Bernard's feelings? So stupid?* Still looking out the window, he said, "This must be as hard for you as it is for me."

"Don't flatter yourself."

Justin turned to him. "I wasn't."

They looked at each other without talking. Justin began to understand how Phoenix felt, how Bernard felt, and how love worked. He laughed. Everything became incredibly simple at that moment. And he accepted Phoenix as Bernard accepted him. He would love Phoenix as much as he ever did and accept the love she offered him. He lit two cigarettes and gave one to Bernard.

"We're romantic fools, Bernard, and we'll suffer for it."

"You heteros can't be trusted."

"I guess I always thought since I'm a man and Phoenix is a woman, then there was always some chance. I didn't mean to trivialize your feelings for me."

"You never did."

"If I offended you in any way, Bernard, I'm sorry."

"I knew what I was getting into. Besides, you're not that far off. There's always that possibility for you and Phoenix, but with you and me... there is none. If you're not gay, you're not gay, and that will never change. I always knew that for me there was no chance."

Justin nodded his head. He knew, now, for him and Phoenix, there was no chance. A familiar pain overtook him for a moment but then peaceably receded.

"I love you, Bernard, you know that."

"I know."

They hugged and said good night. Justin got out and walked upstairs to his loft while Bernard drove down the alley, wanting to cry. Tonight he felt Justin's soul get lighter and it pleased him, but it also pained him because he knew he'd lost him forever as a lover.

When Justin walked into his loft, he saw Dylan's black leather boots next to his black leather Corbusier chaise lounge. He kicked the toe of Dylan's boots and felt the steel there. He saw Dylan's leather jacket on his leather Eileen Gray sofa. When he looked in Phoenix's open bedroom door, he saw Phoenix's face and, nestled next to her, the back of Dylan's head. The sun, shining through the windows, lit upon Phoenix, turning her light brown hair golden and her soft features regal. Under the sheets, their forms looked as one.

The loaded gun hung in his hand as he stood by the door. He pointed the gun at the back of Dylan's head. "Bang," he said softly.

Justin left Phoenix's threshold and went to the kitchen. He poured himself a chilled vodka then sat down at the kitchen table where he unloaded the gun, placing the bullets on the thick glass tabletop.

CHAPTER 27

Fall had arrived in St. Louis and Justin walked on Cherokee Street in the south side of St. Louis surrounded by beautiful dying things. Above him, colorful pear-shaped leaves had started their descent. Behind him were old mansions from the past, and the remains of an old brewery. Under him were the Cherokee caves, where fossils of extinct mammals were once discovered. Last year, Bernard took Justin through an old entrance in the basement of an abandoned building and guided him through the unlit caves. "They were used during Prohibition to smuggle out liquor," he had told him. In front of Justin, his shadow, long on the cement, timed his walk down the tree-lined sidewalk of Cherokee Street. On both sides of Justin, for several blocks, were stores selling furniture of modern antiquity and vintage apparel.

Cars drove slowly up and down what St. Louisans called Antique Row, letting groups of short-sleeved browsers cross the street, or as the drivers themselves tried to look closer at an art deco toaster or some interesting article from the past. A shopkeeper smiled and stopped sweeping his stoop as Justin approached. The sound of the Japanese koto came from inside the shop and the music stayed with Justin for several blocks. Three old women, walking abreast, and busy talking about their grandchildren, walked toward Justin who politely stepped off the sidewalk to let them pass.

He walked aimlessly in and out of the numerous shops. In a small store on the corner, Justin saw an original painting of a Native American who faintly resembled his uncle George Sitting Wolf in Oregon. The painting depicted a young dog warrior of the Southern Cheyenne wearing a feathered headdress and carrying an eagle bone whistle, a rattle of buffalo hooves, and a bow with arrows. It was his uncle who told the young Justin of his noble lineage and direct decadency of chief Dull Knife of the Northern Cheyenne.

"Your great-great-great-great grandfather was chief Morning Star," Sitting Wolf told Justin in the earliest memory Justin had of him. "He was called Dull Knife by the Sioux, but his Cheyenne name was Tahmelapashme. My grandfather was named Ohcumgache, or Little Wolf, in honor of Dull Knife's brother. My father—your grandfather— was called Morning Star. I was named Sitting Wolf and your mother was named Yellow Woman, but she refused to accept it. You were never given a proper Cheyenne name, but it will come to you someday."

"How 'bout Justin Big Tree Climber!" Justin said watching his younger brother trying to climb a tree in the backyard.

"Okay Justin Big Tree Climber."

He was about to leave when his mother walked in. "Why do you tell him all that crap?" she asked. "It doesn't matter anymore. It's ancient history. Can we move on?"

Her brother smiled and said: "He may want to know this someday, sister. If no one is left to tell the story about the Beautiful People who will remember? There'll be no one left to speak their names."

"Nonsense," she said, "Stop perpetuating the myth of our noble race. And get your feet off my coffee table, that cost $700."

"Go on, Big Tree Climber," Sitting Wolf had said, "go climb some big trees."

Justin Sunder remembered his mother's attitude toward Indians even at a young age. He remembered feeling ashamed and embarrassed to look so much like an Indian. But now, looking at the painting, Justin felt the connection to his past and was proud.

"How much is this?" he asked the old woman behind the counter.

"I'm sorry, that's one of the few things in here that's *not* for sale."

Justin smiled. *Yeah,* he thought, *he wouldn't be for sale.* "This looks like my uncle."

"Really?" the woman asked and looked closer at the painting then him. She remarked on the similarities between the brave in the painting and Justin. "It could be," she said. "I wish I could sell it to you, but it was a gift from a friend and we promised not to let it go."

"I respect your loyalty."

Justin thoughts turned back to George. He recalled so many impressions of late, all of which kept pointing to Sitting Wolf. He wondered how difficult his mother would be when he asker her for help in finding him.

He was about to leave Cherokee Street when he happened upon a shop that had a display of glass and marble sculptures. He walked in, and the old man behind the counter looked up. "Evening, young man. Can I help you?"

"I just want to see what you have here," Justin said looking at the sculptured pieces.

"Those are Italian marble and hand-blown glass," the man said with pride. "I got 'em in France."

"It's quite a collection." Justin looked at the pieces, mostly animals and flowers, nothing exciting, but the quality could not be denied. He picked up a few pieces, looking for the seams that were cleverly hidden by the merger of the other images made from a different element. Behind a marble and glass Minotaur was an image Justin immediately recognized. It was the mythological phoenix, displaying a mixture of sorrow and pleasure as she rose from the flames.

The eight-inch bird had remarkable detail. The marble was white Calcutta carefully chiseled so every feather could be counted. Her talons disappeared in hand-blown glass of red and yellow that licked up to the breast. Justin carefully picked it up; it rested lightly in his hands.

"You like that, huh?" the proprietor asked.

"I love it," Justin said, holding the phoenix tenderly in both hands. He turned it over to look for a mark that designated the artist or studio it came from. All he could find was the price tag. *If an artist with a name had the talent to create this piece, it would be worth millions,* Justin thought as he approached the counter. *But this unknown artisan probably died in obscurity.*

"That's $1,200," the old man said, eyeing the longhaired young man over his glasses.

Justin slowly pulled out his wallet. Resting behind his driver's license was the American Express his parents gave him before he left for college. It was about to expire, and for the first time since leaving college, Justin Sunder handed a merchant his credit card.

CHAPTER 28

Justin returned home just before sunset. Phoenix, who had just woke up, poured him a cup of coffee and asked him if he wanted to share her breakfast. Justin declined the offer, sat down on his sofa, and started reading. When Phoenix finished eating, she brought over a mug of coffee and set it down on the end table near his elbow.

"There's a house I heard about, right up your alley, you wanna escort me?"

"No thanks," he said without looking up from his book.

"You and I haven't gone dancing since you picked up that Uzi, aren't you ready for a fix yet?"

"No, I'm not. Take Dylan," he said and the thought—the act—of *not* dancing pleased him.

"I thought, maybe, just you and me could go. You know, like we used to. Remember—"

Justin set his book down and interrupted her, "Phoenix, I don't think I can do this anymore."

"What?" Phoenix asked concerned.

"The dancing. The counting coup on the rich. The stealing. I don't want to be a thief anymore." As Justin spoke, he educed the truth and sincerity from what he finally voiced aloud.

Phoenix sat next to him. She expected something like this to happen and she knew what his words meant. She also knew there was nothing she could do about it. "Why?" she asked softly. Everything was about to change.

Justin took a moment before answering. He expected an argument from Phoenix, but she was surprisingly calm. "It's wrong," he said, rising off the sofa. "It's wrong for me." The words spoken solidified his thoughts. He glanced out the window. The sun had left the Midwest, but its afterglow remained.

"I'm going to make peace with my parents."

"Your parents? What the hell do they have to do with anything?"

"I used to think they were indirectly responsible for my decision to start stealing. I broke into their friends' simplistic mansions of my father's design to show how vulnerable anyone can be. I wanted to prove that even they weren't safely removed from the real world, no matter how many locks they put around themselves. No matter how secure they made themselves feel, they were only locking themselves *in*. I had these crusades against the wealthy.

"Then it diverged: it became guns. And then my reasons split again: it became businesses. When I met you, it changed again. With you, I was dancing for a different reason. I had never met anybody like you before, and I wanted to feel the excitement you felt. I wanted to get closer to you." Justin paused for a moment then continued, "But after a while even that changed. I didn't know what I was doing anymore. After meeting Dylan, I realized, like him, I had no reason. Everything changed again and I didn't know what to do... until recently. Now I know."

Justin took his book and walked into his bedroom, closing his door behind him.

Phoenix watched him walk away, and didn't know what she should do. Whenever she tried to talk to him lately, he was reserved, like a part of his personality had dissolved away. At first, she thought it was because of Dylan, but Justin convinced her it wasn't, so she thought it was her. She wondered what she did to lose her friend and what she could do to get him back.

And now this. He doesn't want to dance anymore!

Whenever they talked, Justin's countenance seemed to Phoenix as boredom. She thought he was bored with her and her conversation, because they never talked, and even with her presence, because he avoided her. She dropped her shoulders and slumped into the sofa as she stared at Justin's closed door.

Later, when Phoenix talked to Dylan, he was understanding at first, but when she talked about her love for Justin and how she was lonely for his friendship, his company, Dylan became angry. *His attitude keeps fuckin' with my relationship with Phoenix*, Dylan thought. *At every turn his bullshit keeps fucking with us.*

On a rare occasion, at Phoenix's encouragement, the two men went out together one evening. Sitting at J.B.'s and not knowing what to talk about, their conversation dragged. Dylan brought up their recent past together but that failed. He asked Justin about his scar, but Justin refused to tell him the story. He asked Justin about Phoenix, but Justin just looked at him and didn't say anything, and Dylan thought he was hiding something. He wondered if Phoenix and Justin had been lovers before he came along and if Justin had feelings for her.

"Did I ever tell you I love her?" Dylan asked.

"No." Justin lit a cigarette.

"No, I guess I never have. I told her, though. She said she loves me, too."

Justin stirred his empty glass, sending the tiny ice cubes at the bottom chasing after each other. When he noticed Dylan's empty beer, he got up to get another round.

At the bar, two men made rude comments about Justin's long braided hair. They insulted him in whispers to each other, but Justin heard them. Even Dylan in the booth could tell by their actions they were insulting Justin.

"Why do you put up with that shit, man?" asked Dylan when Justin returned with the drinks.

"What are you talking about?"

"What do you mean, 'What am I talking about'? That shit from those yuppie-assholes, that's what I'm talking about. Didn't you know they were talking about you?"

"I knew. But you have to pick your fights, Dylan. And I'm not talking about picking fights, I'm talking about choosing the fights you want to be in." He looked around the bar and took a drink. "Besides, people like that aren't going to change by punching them in the head."

"Who wants to change them? I just want them to stay in suburbia where they belong."

"I taught myself a long time ago, Dylan, to walk away. It's just not worth it. When something *needs* to be done, I'll do it, but I refuse to get involved in a fight that merely *wants* to be."

"I understand. It's like me. The fights I get into need to be; they *need* to correct some asshole's thinking. I don't *want* to, but they *need* it just the same. Like those yuppie-assholes at the bar. They *need* their asses kicked. And if you ain't gonna do it, who is?"

Justin, who used to find Dylan's naiveté endearing, now thought it limiting. "It's not the same thing."

Justin looked up when the door opened, hoping whoever was coming in was somebody he knew. But the two men walking in were not people he wanted to talk to anymore than he wanted to continue talking with Dylan. It was David, with Kevin two steps behind him.

The two large men acknowledged Justin with a nod as they walked past.

Justin watched David sign Kevin's name on the chalkboard then sit down on an old church pew facing the pool table. Dylan noticed Justin's gaze.

"What are you looking at?"

"Remember that dance downtown?"

"Yeah."

"That's the guy, David, sitting on the pew with his cue between his legs, next to the girl with the hat on."

Dylan casually turned to look at David, a clean-shaven man with short hair. Dylan had seen him before. David wore a long leather duster, white turtleneck, new jeans, and cowboy boots with silver tips on the toes that sparkled like two little stars. "That's him, huh?"

"He's still looking for us." Justin finished his drink and rose from the booth. "Stay away from that guy."

"Stop telling me what to do, Justin," Dylan said slowly.

"Fine, Dylan. I'm leaving."

"Maybe I'll stick around and play some pool."

"Do whatcha gotta do, man, but I'm telling you: don't mess with this guy."

Dylan twitched and his beer bottle hit the wall, breaking off the tip. "I'm a big boy now, Sunder, I can handle myself. I'm not an idiot that doesn't know what he's doing. I'm getting a little sick of you always acting so superior!"

Justin shook his head and left.

Dylan ordered another beer then walked back to the black chalkboard. After signing his name under Kevin's, he sat next to David on the church pew.

CHAPTER 29

On a warm November night, the nightclub Echo, threw its third anniversary party. The club was one of the few dance clubs Justin, Phoenix, Bernard, and their friends claimed as their own. When it first opened downtown, the owner tried to give it an air of elitism for the small St. Louis underground. He told the doorman to pick people out of line for early admittance, those who deviated from the conservative St. Louis norm in the way they dressed, acted, or looked. After the first month, those previously picked out of the line knew they could confidently walk past the formed line and get in without being carded. The approach worked. Echo became an almost private club; the first nightclub to cater exclusively to a clientele formerly ignored. And it made the owner almost $250,000 in the first year. But in the second year, the owner, in debt due to several expensive habits, told the doorman to let anyone with proper I.D. in, but even proper I.D. became questionable into the third year.

Echo, the first nightclub to open in an area downtown full of deserted brick buildings, was a large, dark box. On its opening night, Justin observed that the name was fitting because everybody had to repeat what they had just said, and everybody said the same thing. And the music, too, echoed in its patron's ears twenty minutes after they had left.

Phoenix and Justin were no longer regulars but they were still considered members of the original family and they, and their entourage, were admitted without waiting in line nor paying a cover.

Justin Sunder wore a red bow tied to the end of his familiar, French braided, raven-black hair. Phoenix, dressed all in white, walked behind him, glowing in the dark club. Her white outfit included a white veil that blurred her face, giving her an ethereal look. When she took a drag off her cigarette, she did so without lifting her shroud. Her red lips and green eyes added soft, muted color to her features. Dylan followed, wearing his familiar uniform: leather boots, jeans, and black motorcycle jacket. Bernard entered and took off his long coat. Some of his friend's by the front door commented on his newest tattoo—an elaborate waterfall crashing from a craggy cliff on his right shoulder, within the cascading water was the image of an Indian brave. Carl and Danny-boy walked in together with their arms around each other. Jeanette, in baggy wool pants, wool topcoat, and fedora, white shirt and tie walked in with Ginny on her arm and the two immediately walked downstairs to find her friend who had mushrooms. Stephanie, the last to enter, was dressed similar to Phoenix but all in red, with her long hair dyed a matching hue. She started dancing as soon as she turned the corner, drawn into the pounding music and flashing lights of the dance floor.

Inside Echo, Justin and the remaining party all gathered at the bar. Waiting for the bartender, Justin leaned against the glass brick bar, which had a light underneath, that made the bar top glow.

Next to Justin stood four men. Justin noticed one of them wore snakeskin cowboy boots and recalled a comment made from Stephanie: "The first time you see a pair of snakeskin cowboy boots in our bar, it's over, We'll all have to find someplace else to get stupid." The man immediately next to Justin looked at his Indian features and held up a hand. "How," he said and his friend, wearing the snakeskin cowboy boots, laughed. Another man, wearing a St. Louis Cardinals baseball cap tried to talk to Phoenix, "Are you an artist? I own a company that might want to buy some art." He hoped she would ask him about his company, but she didn't. Another man turned toward Danny-boy and Carl and noticing Danny-boy's eyeliner and lipstick, and the soft, effeminate features of Carl, moved to the other side of his friends.

The four men turned their attention to two women wearing short leather skirts and knee-high leather boots. All four surrounded the two women and tried to talk to them. One man, wearing an oversized St. Louis Blues hockey jersey, noticed the taller woman wasn't wearing a bra under her unzipped leather jacket. He grabbed her lapel and opened the jacket to show his friends her breasts. The tall woman slapped him, zipped up her jacket, and stormed off. "If she didn't want me to do that, she should've been wearing a bra," he said. His friends laughed and agreed. All four moved to the edge of the dance floor and stood in a dark area just beyond the sweeping lights.

The music, hard and fast, moved everybody on the dance floor: Ministry and Nitzer Ebb were rotated with Erasure and Bananarama. The dancers were washed in multi-colored lights; the artificial fog silhouetted their constantly moving forms. Phoenix moved under the flashing lights that licked her body. The dancers ebbed to the edge of the dance floor and flowed back into the sea of naked arms and legs, catching the bouncing lights like waves. Phoenix joined Stephanie on a raised platform near the wall and the two danced together. Phoenix's eyes flicked in a light that hit her on regular beats.

Justin and Dylan watched the two women from a wooden rail by the dance floor.

Justin saw the angelic image of Phoenix moving with seductive fluidity in the smoking sea. The white of Phoenix and the red of Stephanie mingled like a quivering flame. All of Justin's senses became enhanced. The wooden rail on which his hand rested became hot; he smelled the smoke; he tasted the heat of his cigarette; he heard the fire crackling in the music and the talk. And he saw Phoenix moving in the flame.

Dylan saw them dancing and clutched the rail. Phoenix's hands traveled down Stephanie's hips and the two danced like lovers, lost in the smoke and the lights and the music. Dylan watched them dancing and became jealous of Stephanie touching Phoenix's body with such familiarity. He thought about breaking them up.

Bernard approached Justin, "Jeanette scored some 'shrooms. You guys want in?"

"Sure," said Justin, who wanted to remove himself from the fire. He motioned to Dylan, who reluctantly followed.

The party gathered in a corner commons area full of colorful, squat furniture from the old St. Louis Insane Asylum. The chairs and settees were big with rounded edges and heavy bases. Jeanette, in a hard plastic chair, sat next to Danny-boy and Carl. Justin sat in a chair behind a thick wooden pillar that blocked his view of Phoenix. Dylan stood just at the edge of their enclave, watching the dancers. Ginny sat on the floor at Jeanette's feet, and Bernard leaned against the pillar next to Justin.

"Where's Phoenix and Stephanie?" Jeanette asked. "Somebody grab 'em."

Dylan left immediately and within minutes returned with the two smiling women.

"What's this I hear?" Phoenix exclaimed.

The party settled in and prepared to eat the 'shrooms. Anticipating the unpleasant tasting and dry hallucinogenic, all took a sip from their drinks to numb their palates and moisten their mouths. They ate the drug quickly, chewing just enough to send it down their throats. After each swallow, they chased it with their drinks to reduce the aftertaste.

Dylan ate his share then excused himself to go to the bathroom where he planned to shove his finger down his throat.

After eating the mushrooms, the party dispersed and roamed throughout the club, stopping to talk casually with friends and strangers. They discussed the different drugs circulating around the club, the people they liked or didn't like, the music that played or should be playing; they talked about the night before, clothes, sex. They danced, together or alone, whenever and wherever the mood swayed them. They sought out certain people and tried to avoid others. Scattered around the club, they drank, they laughed, and all waited for the drug to take effect.

On the dance floor, Carl interrupted Phoenix and Stephanie dancing together just long enough to give them both a kiss, and then danced off. After Carl left, two men, who had been watching the women playfully dancing with each other, crossed the wooden floor and approached them.

"Hi," one man said, attempting to dance with Phoenix. "My name's Robert, what's yours?" He clumsily stepped on her foot with his snakeskin cowboy boots. "Sorry," he said. Phoenix said something he didn't hear. "Can I buy you a drink?" he asked.

Phoenix continued to dance with Stephanie who had a baseball cap hovering over her. "You from New York?" asked the face under the cap who then tapped her on the shoulder and asked, "You with that ginger?" He thumbed toward Carl.

"Yes."

"Why?"

"Are you two bi?" Robert asked Phoenix. "I know a girl that's bi—"

Phoenix turned to him. "Drop the fuck off!" she said and both Stephanie and Phoenix walked off the dance floor.

When the toxins of the mushrooms started altering their senses, they all gently started converging from all corners of the club back to the oversized furniture. Justin commented on the synchronicity of the event. The commons area was full, but Stephanie, Danny-boy, and Carl found an unoccupied settee and sat down. Just then, a man got out of a big yellow chair, and Dylan dragged the bulky seat over for Phoenix. She sat down and Dylan sat on the armrest. Justin sat with crossed legs and a straight spine at Phoenix's feet. Ginny laid down in the middle of the gathering, her limbs draped on the people near her. Bernard and Jeanette leaned on the armrests of the settee.

Stephanie leaned over and chewed on Phoenix's ear. "How's your new boy?" she asked. "He has bad-boy, good-sex all over him."

"You're wrong." Phoenix smiled.

"What, the bad-boy or the good-sex?"

"The bad-boy."

Stephanie laughed and pointed at Dylan's crotch. "Bad boy!" she said. "Let me have a go at him."

"I don't share."

"Yes you do."

"Not this one."

"He's your property?"

"I've marked him."

Slowly the group began to talk as one. Their sentences broken, as if every word took on the meaning of ten. When a man—who Phoenix recognized by face only—walked by, she said to Stephanie, "Searching."

"Always looking," said Stephanie.

"Lost," added Dylan.

"Adrift," said Jeanette.

"He just waves," Carl said.

"Even when he talks, he's just waving," said Bernard.

"These are great," Dylan said. "I'm tripping my brains out."

Phoenix touched his ear. "Yuck." She wiped her hand off on her leg and laughed.

Every now and then people stopped by, but when the music called or they saw another group of people they knew, they'd jump up and be off again. The group saw an endless train of shadowed people with familiar faces whose names they'd forgotten.

The party fused together, finishing each other's sentences and even, occasionally, their thoughts. Dylan, who ate less 'shrooms then the others, was more coherent and in control. He often had to remind someone where they were in their story that branched off in sporadic tales.

At one point, Dylan, who had been watching the dancers, said, "Don't it look like those dancers are being shot by those lights?"

Bernard laughed and said, "Yeah, they're being jerked around by the impact."

Phoenix said, "And they call it dancing."

"Yeah, but they're really being shot."

"The lights are guns."

"Their lights are bullets."

Justin didn't think the lights were shooting the dancers at all; he thought the laser lights were sculpting them, etching their form and giving them life.

As the effect of the drug became stronger in Justin, the quieter he became. And then suddenly he felt the need to be alone. He stood up and walked away. His friends didn't think anything of it until an hour later when Phoenix asked if anybody had seen Justin. Nobody had. She then asked several people in the bar. No one knew. Finally, she asked the doorman and he told her Justin had left.

CHAPTER 30

The stars offered inspiration for Justin and he absorbed their wisdom of the velvet night like a vessel as he walked 12 city blocks to the bank of the Mississippi River.

As he walked the streets, the city opened up before him and in his mind's eye he saw a heavily wooded area he knew to be Oregon. In a clearing, he saw his uncle, wearing a hat with two buffalo horns and sitting beside a fire, smoking tobacco from an old deer bone pipe. He saw a round tepee he knew to be a sweat lodge, erected near a cool blue river. A trail led from the river to the fire to the sweat lodge. He heard birds nearby. And chanting in the fire. He knew his uncle had been fasting. As Justin drew closer Sitting Wolf asked him, "Where do you want to live?" Justin sat beside his uncle who then offered him the pipe.

"With you."

"Where do you want to live?"

"Here, with you."

"Where do you want to live?"

I don't understand. I don't know.

The river in Oregon slowly became larger, the landscape faded from brilliant to bleak, the serenity was replaced with city noises, and Justin suddenly found himself sitting on the western bank of the Mississippi River. He watched the undaunted river pass at his feet. Twenty yards out, the river rumbled over some unseen obstacle. Justin watched a piece of wood bounce in the current as it passed. Fifty yards out, the smooth river reflected the soft moonlight. A 100 yards out, a small island challenged the strong river and stood alone. Past the island, Justin looked at the dark eastern shoreline. He pulled the bow out of his hair. He imagined he could throw it over the river, past the island, all the way to the other side. The wind blew just as he let go and the red bow landed in the dark water at his feet.

Justin stood at the dirty river's edge, looking up at the sky. The moon was full and low. The smell of stagnant mud and decaying fish permeated the air. In Oregon, Sitting Wolf had 180 acres 20 minutes from the Pacific. He had a plantation where he grew birches, pines and red cedars, along with cultivating florae being destroyed by deforestation, and he grew medicinal herbs. Justin's uncle arrived shortly after Justin had been badly burned, carrying a medicine bag of balsam fir oleoresin, witch hazel leaves and bark, and sedative herbs of California poppy and Virginia skullcap, cannabis, and other healing herbs. Sitting Wolf and his medicine was scoffed at by the Sunder family and their doctors and was never given a chance to help heal Justin's wound.

Justin thought of healing; then remembered the vision of his uncle asking him:

"Where do you want to live?"

Where indeed, Justin thought, finally understanding the question wasn't referring to a physical place but rather a metaphysical one. *Where do I want to live? Not where I am.*

Justin lifted himself from the riverbed and returned home to write to Sitting Wolf. Last week he had called his mother and after a short, polite conversation, he finally got to the point and asked for his uncle's address.

"Good Lord, now you wanna go and be an Indian in Oregon?"

"Better that than one living in denial." The conversation ended soon after.

After Justin got home he wrote a letter to his uncle; then sat down in his indoor garden and began to prune. While he pruned he occasionally glanced at all the things he and Phoenix had in their loft: the prints, paintings, furniture, television, stereo, even the damn toaster—all stolen; the rugs, the answering machine, even the things bought, like the curtains that blew beside his garden, the mulch, the seeds—were all bought with stolen money. The things that were not acquired dishonestly or illegally were given to him by his parents, or bought by his parents' credit card (he thought about the marble and glass phoenix). His eyes searched the loft for *one* item he had earned honestly on his own.

Inside club Echo, Bernard, Phoenix and Dylan sat in the corner commons area, talking about Justin. When the conversation turned to his mastery of the lock, Phoenix talked about his skills in the past tense. Bernard spoke affectionately of Justin while Dylan attempted—unsuccessfully—to guile Phoenix and Bernard into acknowledging Justin's faults.

Suddenly a man landed into their table, his baseball cap with the logo of the St. Louis Cardinals rolled by Dylan's feet. He landed on Phoenix, who was knocked over with a loud thud. Following him into the fray was a tall skinhead who had just been insulted by the Cardinal fan. Phoenix tried to crawl away as the two men fought practically on top of her.

In an instant Dylan snapped. He jumped up, grabbed a beer bottle and cracked it over the tattooed head, picked him up, and tossed him aside. Phoenix scuttled away to safety. Blind with anger, Dylan attacked the man who had landed on her. His hard hands, knotted with rage, slammed into the clean-shaven face. Blood quickly covered his knuckles.

When Dylan threw the skinhead, he landed on a pair of snakeskin cowboy boots. Still stunned from the bottle Dylan had broken over his head, he stumbled as an unknown assailant struck him repeatedly. A second skinhead grabbed Dylan who quickly broke free and punched him straight in the face, sending him into the man wearing the St. Louis Blues jersey. The two fraternities began to brawl, hitting anybody who looked different from them. And in the middle of it all, with no allegiance to any faction, was Dylan attacking anybody who opposed him. His adrenaline surged and—like a feral animal—he smelled blood and fear.

The bouncers, who always welcomed a fight in their bar, ran over to break it up. They busted into the conflict and commanded instant respect. Most stopped fighting with each other and were easily controlled. Two large security guards easily pushed the five men who had been fighting out the door, the crowd immediately parting for them. But Dylan took the concentrated effort of the biggest bouncer. The two men pulled, pushed, dragged, and thumped each other as they tried to gain dominance over the other. It was only after another bouncer returned to help his comrade were they able to throw Dylan out into the streets. He stumbled and fell onto the cracked cement but jumped up quickly. The biggest bouncer hit Dylan square in the chest, sending him back to the pavement.

Bernard had followed Dylan outside, and after the bouncers walked back into the club, he helped him up. Dylan stopped fighting but was still shaking with rage.

"Motherfucker! God-damn-motherfucker! Where is the son of a bitch? I'll kill 'em!" Motherfucker! Where is she? Where's Phoenix? Son of a bitch! Is she okay? Did you see those motherfuckers land on her? Where is she?"

"She's fine, Dylan. She's fine." Bernard saw the madness in his eyes, the vacant stare with clear determination. Even his breath smelled foul for a moment. "She's fine, Dylan."

"I don't take shit from nobody and nobody fucks with me or mine!" Dylan began to pace and Bernard tried to calm him down.

"Phoenix is inside," Bernard said. "She's fine."

Dylan stopped walking. He leaned against the wall. "She's okay?" he asked, looking around as if for the first time.

"Yes."

They both leaned against the wall, and Dylan started to relax.

"Man, you fucking exploded," Bernard said.

Dylan exhaled loudly. He looked at his hands that began to tremble less and less the more he came out of fury.

"You okay?" Bernard asked.

"I'm okay."

"Phoenix doesn't like violence, Dylan. When she comes out, you'd better be cool."

"I'm cool," Dylan said as if waking from a deep sleep.

A few minutes later Phoenix walked out of the bar, followed by her friends.

"Wow, I can't handle that right now," Stephanie said.

"Little boys, violent little boys everywhere," said Phoenix. She had retreated to the bar, refusing to watch the rumble. She was there when Danny-boy came up to inform her Dylan had been thrown out.

Carl approached Bernard, "What a buzz kill." Jeanette, who watched the fight with pleasure, didn't think it was a buzz kill at all.

Dylan, whose hair was tangled and face flushed approached Phoenix and kissed her. Phoenix, seeing Dylan's disheveled appearance, hugged him and asked, "You okay?"

"I'm fine."

"What happened?"

"I don't know. I didn't do anything, next thing I knew, I'm in the middle of a fight. I'm getting hit, trying to defend myself," Dylan said wiping his bloody knuckles onto his jeans, "and before I know it, I'm being thrown out on the streets."

Bernard looked at Dylan and wondered how he could be so calm, so quickly, after being so fierce. And he no longer trusted him. Ginny and Danny-boy, who saw the whole fight, knew Dylan was lying but said nothing.

"Let's get out of here," said Dylan, and taking Phoenix's hand he headed toward the parking lot. The entourage followed.

CHAPTER 31

Just before Christmas, a photograph of his uncle standing by a small river in the woods arrived in the mail for Justin. On the reverse, Sitting Wolf simply wrote: "You're welcome at my home anytime, Justin. A place is being made ready for you."

Justin immediately called his uncle. Sitting Wolf talked softly and unhurriedly to his nephew. Toward the end of the 20 minute conversation, George told Justin he could stay as long as he wanted. He then gave Justin directions to his cabin in southern Oregon.

"I'll see you in a month," Justin said.

"I'm proud of you, son. You have the blood of Tahmelapashme and Ohcumgache in you, and they've been calling you home. I'll see you soon."

Justin Sunder spent the next couple of days getting everything in order: changing the name on the lease, phone bill, and utilities from Justin Sunder to Phoenix... Sunder. Justin—not knowing her last name and the landlord and utility companies' refusal to accept a single name on a bill—gave her his last name, literally and forever. He would not call himself a Sunder again. It was difficult for Justin to face her and tell her he was leaving so he avoided her as much as he could. He knew she'd be upset and he wasn't sure he had the strength to turn away: he desperately needed to be strong.

One early evening, while he was making a list of several personal items he wanted to sell, items that wouldn't affect Phoenix's quality of life, she showed up unexpectedly. Justin wanted to leave the room because, in an instant, he saw her more beautiful than ever before. She dyed her shoulder-length hair red, and it fell around her golden face, framing her jade eyes. Justin got out of his chair and walked into his bedroom.

Phoenix had had enough. "Stop!" she yelled. "Justin, please stop," she added softly. He obeyed. "Why don't you talk to me?"

He turned toward her. "What do you want to talk about?"

"What's going on with you? We don't hang out anymore. We don't talk anymore. We don't do anything together. What happened?"

Justin didn't know how to answer. Where to begin. The moment he feared had arrived. "It's time for me to make some changes," he said, his face devoid of emotion.

Phoenix realized those changes didn't include her. They stared at each other for a long time; Justin gathered strength in the silence, while Phoenix tried to put all the pieces together. And Phoenix thought she understood.

"You don't love me anymore," she said and tears came to her eyes. She hadn't meant to say "love" but now, after saying it, the word seemed right.

Justin looked into Phoenix's eyes that began to glisten from the sunset and saltwater. "How can you say that?" he asked with a shaky voice that he hoped she didn't notice.

"Then why do you shut me out like this? What did I do?"

It was the "what did I do?" that almost made Justin cry. "Phoenix..." he began, but had to stop himself. He swallowed, widened his eyes, and then looked away. "I'm sorry, Phoenix. It's not you." Justin paused. "It's me. I'm not happy."

"Why are you not happy? What changes do you have to make? Talk to me, Justin. You're not as ignorant as you're pretending to be; you know what's making you unhappy. You know what changes you must make. Why won't you talk to me? Goddamn it!"

Justin paused for a moment then summed everything up by telling her he was leaving.

Phoenix looked at him. Her shoulders dropped. "Leaving," she said. In an instant, she saw herself utterly alone. "Me or St. Louis?"

"I'm going to Oregon to stay with my uncle."

She felt weak and had trouble walking into her bedroom. She closed the door and sat on her bed. "Leaving," she said to herself. The word embodied so much meaning for Phoenix that it became something abstract. "Leaving."

Justin returned to her bedroom after a few minutes. When he entered, he stood in silence. Phoenix looked up. *How empty her face looks*, Justin thought, *how tragic and beautiful*.

"Can we go with you?" Phoenix softly asked.

Justin bowed his head and took a step toward the window.

"Me. I. Can I go with you?"

Justin walked to the window and stared out into the alley. The sun had dropped behind the horizon, but the streetlights still hadn't switched on yet. The streets were dark and everything looked gray. Winter had set in.

"I'm sorry," he answered.

"You can't leave me!"

He crossed to the bed and sat next to her. "You'll be fine, Phoenix. You have Dylan now. I know you love him and I know how important that is to you."

"I love you, Justin."

"You love Dylan in a way you could never love me."

"Dylan's not you. It's different. One's not more or less than the other. They're just different."

"I know," Justin said, getting off the bed. "I've been wanting to leave for a long time, I just didn't know it. And now that you have Dylan and you're happy, I can stop worrying about you," he said, hoping not to be condescending, hoping it was brevity to smooth over the pain.

"Worry about me? What about us?"

"We'll always have St. Louis." He smiled.

"Is this a joke? Fuck you!"

"I'm sorry."

Phoenix sat there quietly, trying to control her emotions. Finally she said: "It *is* because of Dylan. And not in the 'now I can stop worrying about you' way. Not in a good way." Phoenix looked up at him defiantly. "Right?" Justin didn't answer. "I have to know."

Justin sat down at her feet and looked up at her. "It has nothing to do with Dylan."

"But Oregon? Your uncle? You never mentioned it before."

"He's my mother's brother, full-blooded Cheyenne. I want to get back to my roots, understand my past, understand my future. This may sound silly but I want his spiritual guidance. I want to do a vision quest and decide what I should do with my life, what direction I should take. Stealing isn't it, school isn't it, and, as much as I love you, my love for you isn't it." Justin paused, waiting for her response but Phoenix just sat there. He noticed her fingers were moving as if she were playing her saxophone. "I'm going to Oregon in a few weeks. Phoenix, I hope you will come out and visit me."

"Justin...." Phoenix didn't know what to say.

"This isn't easy, Phoenix," Justin said knowing after he left he'd probably never see her again. The thought of that, always in his mind, crippled him.

CHAPTER 32

Dylan Panicosky casually drove his new truck through his neighborhood of South City, taking random turns, until finally he ended up at Phoenix's. He'd called her earlier that night and gotten the answering machine. After waiting an hour for her to return the call, he decided to take his black Chevy out for a drive. When Dylan pulled down the alley, he saw Justin in the window of Phoenix's bedroom. Justin, obviously emotional, was standing there talking to someone who Dylan assumed could only be Phoenix.

He wondered what Justin was doing in his girlfriend's bedroom, and what they could be talking about. He turned off the lights and continued down the shadowed alley.

Under the full moon and the dark gray sky, Dylan parked his truck next to a dumpster and watched the window.

"Everything will be told tonight," he said in his dark metal cocoon. *They both have been acting strange lately,* he said to himself as he turned down the radio. He waited and watched as he anticipated Phoenix walking into the frame of the window. He'd understand everything then.

When Phoenix appeared in the window frame, she was completely illuminated. From the back lighting of the room, contrasted with the darkness of the back alley, Dylan could see the theater in her bedroom play out clearly.

Dylan observed Phoenix hug Justin. Hug him and give him a kiss! He watched her press against him and kiss him! Justin held her tight for a long time and kissed her on the neck—*like a lover would do,*

Dylan thought. He scrutinized their embrace, each more reluctant to let go than the other. They kissed again and hugged again and Dylan, suddenly incensed with jealousy and overtaken by rage, punched his hand almost through the driver's side window.

When he saw Justin offer a token of his love—some figurine—that sealed it in Dylan's seething mind: *Justin and Phoenix are having an affair. That's why she didn't return my call tonight! She'd made plans to be with Justin!*

Gravel flew as Dylan sped off down the alley, unaware his knuckles were bleeding.

Justin, hearing the noise down in the alley, looked out the window but only saw an unfamiliar black truck, without its headlights on, rush past and out of sight.

Dylan once again traveled the city streets, driving recklessly, without purpose. Dylan drove his new truck through the projects and through private streets, convinced he was played for a fool.

His mind worked the whole scenario out: Justin and Phoenix were lovers and he was there to make Justin jealous. Phoenix loved Justin, and he was just a pawn! What a laugh Justin must be having now! Justin, the scar-faced punk, who thought he was better than everybody else, only pretended to be a friend so he could show off his intelligence to win Phoenix back! Justin did everything he could to jeopardize and sabotage his relationship with Phoenix.

"I told you not to fuck with me or mine," Dylan said to Justin's image somewhere beyond the glass of the front windshield; he drove as if to run it over.

When Dylan finally realized his knuckles were bleeding he turned into a bar to bandage it up. At first, he didn't realize he was back in Soulard, at J.B.'s.

After Dylan walked in, he saw David and Kevin, standing tall and lit from some unknown light, talking to a blond in a short plastic dress. On his way to the bathroom, Dylan stopped for a second and whispered into David's ear. A few minutes later David followed him into the bathroom. David listened as Dylan, washing and dressing his wounds, talked.

CHAPTER 33

David, sitting next to the quiet blond in the plastic dress, turned to Kevin and asked, "What do you know about that guy Dylan?"

"Supposed to be a Four Horseman. Dates that babe, Phoenix."

David knew the Four Horseman. When he first moved to St. Louis he had had a brief run-in with several of its members over a crystal meth deal that went bad. In David's mind, Dylan's credibility rose. "What about Justin? Remember him?"

"The dude with the burn?"

"Yeah, the dude with the fucking burn!"

"Nothing, really."

"Did Justin *dance* in my apartment?" David asked.

"Dance?"

"Rip me off."

"I don't know, man. It's possible."

"Well, from what Dylan just told me, I think it's very possible."

Kevin recalled a conversation he had had several months ago. "Ya know, I was out with Bernard and Sandy one night when you were out of town and Sandy brought up Phoenix, said she might have done it. She said she'd a rumor that Phoenix was a thief. Since her and Justin are so tight, Justin might have been—"

David interrupted, "Why am I just now hearing about this, Kevin?"

"Bernard said she didn't steal anymore," Kevin quickly continued, realizing he'd made a big, and possibly dangerous, mistake. "He said she was just a petty thief, a shoplifter. He said it so casually, so convincing, ya know? I believed him. Then he told us that even if Phoenix had the skills to pull it off, she couldn't have because they were all down at the lake that weekend. I knew they were friends; it seemed possible that they would go down to the Ozarks together. He made this big thing out of it. He said Justin was there, a couple of other people I don't know... He told me stories about their weekend... It just seemed so real."

"He elaborated on a story you didn't ask him about? That should've been your first clue, Kevin."

"I trusted him, you know? I'm sorry, I never thought he'd lie to you."

"He didn't lie to me. He lied to you," David said as he reached for his pager. "Leave Bernard out of this for now. I'll deal with him later."

"Do you think Bernard told Justin about your stash?"

"I don't think Bernard would be stupid enough to stick around if he had, but he knows something."

"What do you want to do about Phoenix?"

"Her name keeps popping up. If she had a part in this then we'll have fun with her later."

A half-hour later Justin entered J.B.'s

In the back, Kevin nudged David. "Well, well, well, David said." We're fucking blessed, my friend."

"It Was a Very Good Year" began playing as Justin sat at the bar. He grabbed a pen and a clean napkin.

John, wearing a T-shirt with Buck Rogers shooting his ray gun, approached Justin. "You sure are pissing a lot in my bar lately."

"I could go someplace else," Justin said and forced a smile.

"Eh, nobody else would have you." John walked over to the cooler and grabbed the bottle of chilled vodka while Justin started writing a note on the bar napkin. When John returned with two shots, Justin picked up his glass and noticed the vodka was chilled.

"I decided to keep a bottle frozen," John said and winked. "Cheers!"

"To Oregon!"

"To *Oregon*? The state? Or is that some Indian word?"

"Well, yeah, both."

"Okay, what about it?"

"That's where I'm moving to."

"When?"

"Couple of weeks."

"For good?"

Justin nodded.

"Well to hell with you Mister! You been coming in here all these years and then you announce suddenly—just like that—you're leaving? When were you going to tell me?"

"I wouldn't have left without saying good bye, John."

"It just seems kind of sudden, that's all. Is Phoenix going with you?"

"No."

"Well, goddamn it, Justin. I'll miss you! I mean that. You're alright, always have been."

They did another shot and toasted again. "Good luck to you, my friend!" John said.

"Thank you, my friend." Justin said then turned his head to see David and Kevin staring at him. David nodded at Justin and smiled. It was a bad omen, he thought. He said good-bye to John and walked out of J.B.'s for the last time.

A few minutes later, John said good night to David and Kevin.

Outside, walking home, Justin looked up at the night's sky above St Louis; he thought about the sky over Oregon and wondered how many more stars he'd see there. He'd been in rural areas before and was amazed by the beauty of the firmament the further he moved away from Man. The night was calm; the breeze from the afternoon had stopped. It was a steel gray night, and the headlights from the few passing cars shone with extra brilliance.

He thought about his love for Phoenix and decided since he was leaving and had nothing to lose, he'd profess his love for her once more and ask her to come with him. He'd make sure she understood he still loved her and he always would. He wouldn't lie about that anymore. Maybe, while he was gone, she'd realized she loved him; maybe, when he got home tonight, she'd tell him that. Maybe they would make love and fall asleep in each other's arms. And in the morning he'd fix her breakfast. They'd leave St. Louis together. He knew she would welcome the journey he offered. They wouldn't have to go to Oregon, they could go anywhere.

He was thinking about the future with Phoenix when car lights lit him from behind.

Justin heard the rev of an engine and as he turned he heard the squeal of brakes. Then, suddenly, a sharp pain in his leg, and a dull throb in his head.

Semi-conscious, Justin felt himself being picked up. He knew a car had just hit him but he thought it was an accident. He felt himself being thrown roughly onto a seat but he thought he was being helped. When he felt his finger get slammed in the door, he screamed. For just a second Justin regained consciousness. He looked up and saw David smiling.

CHAPTER 34

After Dylan Panicosky left J.B.'s, he decided to drive around the city and collect his thoughts. He drove, this time, stopping at the lights, offering the right-of-way, obeying the speed limit. Across the Mississippi River, he pulled into the parking lot of a nightclub and parked. It started to snow. He watched people come and go, single men and women, couples, groups of men, groups of women. He counted the people entering the club and subtracted that from the people leaving. When the number reached zero, he decided to go confront Phoenix.

He drove fast, with purpose, taking a direct line to Phoenix. When she opened the door, she hugged him and drew him inside. She still held Justin's present, the sculpted phoenix rising from the flames. She told him about Justin's plans to leave and then handed him Justin's old lock-pick set. "A going-away present for you," she told him. "From Justin."

"When did all this happen?"

"Tonight."

And Dylan realized what he witnessed in the window was a farewell scene. He recognized the figurine as the one he saw from the alley. Dylan looked at the lock-pick set resting in his bandaged hand. "Are you going with him?"

"No, he didn't even ask. I'm staying with you."

"Do you love him?"

"Why are you asking me that now?"

"I want to know how you feel about him; how you feel about me."

"I love him but I'm *in* love with you, okay? Don't do this insecure, jealousy, bullshit with me, Dylan. It makes you ugly."

Dylan sat there, silent, thinking about what he'd done. Phoenix, misunderstanding his sullen mood, apologized and asked about his hand. He answered her with a kiss and left. Phoenix, thinking she'd hurt Dylan's feelings, but too tired to handle two problems at once, picked up the sax and played, forcing her emotions through the reed.

Dylan Panicosky returned to J.B.'s and walked through the door just before closing time. He didn't know what he would say to David once he found him, but he knew he had to say something to convince him it was a mistake. He thought about threatening him with the Four Horsemen if he didn't back off. He hoped he wasn't too late. He vowed that if he saw Justin, he would stay up all night protecting him from David. He swore on his brother's grave that if any harm came to Justin, David would pay.

He didn't find Justin or David at J.B.'s. Just as he was turning to leave, he saw the woman in the plastic dress who was with David earlier and approached her. "Where's David?" he demanded.

"He's gone."

"Where did he go?"

"Someplace to talk to somebody about something."

Bitch! "Can I get a hold of him?"

"I don't know."

"Doesn't he have a beeper or something?"

"I don't know," she said and walked away.

Bitch!

Dylan got into his truck and drove around. He tried to think of the places Justin had talked about: the bars in Soulard, the nightclubs downtown, the late-night diners scattered throughout the city, Forest Park in the Central West End, Bernard's apartment in Tower Grove. St. Louis suddenly became huge; Justin could be anywhere. Dylan spent the rest of the night driving, vainly searching for Justin whom he'd betrayed. He called Phoenix periodically to see if Justin had returned.

At the end of his search, he went home, unable to face Phoenix. He fed Law and cleaned up after his father. Unable to sleep, he cleaned the entire house, waking his father when he started vacuuming. When the early light of dawn crept across the Panicoskys' house, Dylan was taking a bath. The snow had stopped and the yards outside had only a fine white mist over them. The roads and the rooftops were clear. From the bathroom window, Dylan saw a black and white view of the world.

In the morning, he got a call from Phoenix who had also been up all night. "Justin," she said in a hollow voice, "was found dead in an alley on the north side."

Dylan, suddenly exhausted, forced himself to drive over to Phoenix's where he stayed up with her until both, weak and tired, escaped into sleep.

Several hours later, Dylan awoke, made himself a sandwich, then entered Justin's room and looked around his sparse, private place. In the closet, he found Justin's collection of firearms. Dylan looked at the rifles, pistols, semi-automatic and automatic guns. He picked up the Uzi and noticed cement was in its barrel. A closer inspection of the other guns revealed the same thing. Except for a 9mm Smith and Wesson, they all had cement poured down their barrels.

"Why would you ruin all these guns?" Dylan asked the empty room.

CHAPTER 35

The wake was held in Kansas City. Many St. Louisans had driven the breadth of Missouri to pay their respects. Bernard was down in Mexico and couldn't be reached. Justin's friends were reserved and polite, but the group, in one way or another, offended the Sunder's and their invited guests. The red hair of Phoenix; the hairstyle or length of the others, seemed inappropriate to them; the partially visible tattoos of some, grotesque; the clothing, although properly black, was too casual or in poor taste. They thought Carl was a homosexual, and couldn't understand why Jeanette dressed like a man. Dylan was the only exception, who had bought an expensive black suit and new shoes for the occasion. John, dressed in his best mourning suit, did not impress the Sunders, who thought him ignorant. The Sunders wondered what kind of life their son had lived in St. Louis.

The small, loyal group met Justin's wealth and took an immediate dislike to his parent's, their friends, and Justin's old Kansas City friends. In the back of the funeral home, during the wake, Stephanie observed a man talking on a cellular phone.

Phoenix met George Sitting Wolf and the two talked as if they had known each other for years.

"I don't know what to do, George" Phoenix confided. "I feel so alone, so empty."

"He was the last of a great line," he said. "There are holes caused by this death." George gazed past Phoenix and for a moment she thought his image had actually blurred, as if he had gone someplace else. He wiped his eyes and gazed upon Phoenix. "He told me many things about you. You had quite a pull on him." Phoenix leaned into his arms and cried. Dylan walked out, saw her crying, and started to go to her, but Sitting Wolf glared at him, and he stopped. "You are welcomed to visit me if you ever find yourself needing sanctuary."

After the funeral, Mrs. Sunder pulled Phoenix aside to give her the note Justin had written that fatal night at J.B.'s.

"The police gave us the things in his pockets," she told Phoenix. "He still had his car keys with him and since I don't need a Nova I thought you might, so here." She paused for a moment then added, "Also, there was a note for you. On a bar napkin." Mrs. Sunder gave her the wrinkled-up napkin. "Poor Justin, he just didn't know... You're such a beautiful girl, he didn't know..." She tried to speak, and Phoenix wanted her to hurry up and spit it out so she could read the note that was absorbing the sweat from her hands. "He just never accepted his scar, you understand, but I hope you accept his note and not think him a fool. He probably really did love you, and I'm sure somewhere he thought you might love him, too. It's a hell of a way to start the New Year, huh? Have pity on his memory, Phoenix, he just didn't know."

"He knew a lot more than you'll ever know," Phoenix said and walked away.

In their hotel room overlooking the Missouri River, Dylan slept and Phoenix read Justin's note again:

Phoenix,
I will always dream
For your whisper of love
To raise my soul
From sleep.

Phoenix watched Dylan sleep, thinking how much he resembled Justin. She never saw it before, but now, clearly, they could have been brothers. Dylan's hair was shorter but the same raven black color; she remembered their eyes, clear, bright white surrounding the dark iris and ebony pupils, were also similar; the high cheekbones; the strong jaw line; the shapely, pronounced lips over the perfect white teeth; the noses, both the same size and length, even the nostrils curved out in the same way. Justin was taller and thinner than Dylan but their bodies, too, had a similar shape. The aura of Dylan seemed to morph into that of Justin's before her very eyes.

Phoenix lightly touched his face and was slightly surprised when Dylan awoke.

"What?"

"I want to go visit Justin."

"Can't we do that in the morning?"

"I'm going now. Do you want to come with me?"

Dylan got up slowly. "Sure, honey."

At the graveyard, Dylan drove the narrow cement road, through the maze of granite and limestone vaults and decorative tombstones, past the manicured lawn, occasionally passing a leafless tree—its stark bareness silhouetted in the night—and found Justin Sunder's large, above-ground memorial next to his brother Matthew's equally impressive vault. Both tombs were of the same design: rounded half-hemispherical mosaic domes, intricate arabesque pendentive, smooth limestone walls, and composite portico. Phoenix had learned a great deal about architecture and design from Justin and thought he'd be pleased. The vaults stood side by side like a mirrored image.

Phoenix got out of the truck, and Dylan, out of respect, left her alone with Justin. The cool night air became warmer as she approached where Justin was laid to rest. She stood at the entrance for a moment before going in and looked up at the constellations. Never before had she understood Justin's fascination with the stars until now. Suddenly she saw the heavens, endless and immortal, as a depository for all knowledge. She imagined the heavens using the stars, like a great sieve, to filter through that knowledge to Man and she wondered if maybe the artificial lights of the city and pollution blocked that sieve where the icons of Man's achievements and intelligence actually closed the fountainhead and stagnated Man.

She lowered her eyes to Justin's vault. His portrait was engraved in stone above the entrance, minus the scar. The absence of the scar disturbed her. It didn't seem right that the mark, that defined him and gave him strength, should be missing. Phoenix blinked her eyes and entered.

"You love Dylan in a way you could never love me," she remembered him saying, and her response, "Dylan's not you. It's different, one's not more or less than the other. They're just different." And she recalled now how heavy his words had sounded when he answered, "I know."

"I do love you, Justin," Phoenix said, and her words echoed slightly in the half-enclosed tomb, moot words in a stone hall falling on dead ears. "God, do you know how this hurts?" She started to cry again, tried to stop, then relinquished all control to her emotions. She slid down the wall in a fetal position and cried until she fell asleep.

An hour later Dylan walked in and saw Phoenix asleep with streaks of dried tears on her cheeks. He picked her up and carried her to his truck. After covering her with a blanket, he went back to Justin's tomb. The relief image of Justin's face carved above the entrance stopped Dylan for a moment. He had to force himself to enter the quiet structure. Inside, his steps were labored. When he reached Justin, he touched the cold stone. "I'm sorry, Justin, I'm sorry," he repeated over and over. "I should have trusted you. I should have trusted Phoenix." He lamented over that night. He cursed himself. "You were my friend and I killed you and I killed a part of Phoenix." In the dark vault he vowed: "And now I'm going to kill David!" As soon as they got back to St. Louis, Dylan promised, David would die.

CHAPTER 36

They left Kansas City in the morning, without a word between them, and headed back to St. Louis. For 126 miles they drove east on highway 70; Dylan, lost in his own thoughts of regret and revenge, said little during the drive home, and Phoenix, with no thoughts at all, welcomed the silence. Just outside of Columbia, they acknowledged they were both hungry and stopped at a truck stop for breakfast.

While waiting for their food to arrive, Phoenix lit a cigarette and asked, "What do you think we should do?"

"About what?"

Phoenix shrugged her shoulders. "I don't know, with our lives?"

"What can we do? We can only try to enjoy ourselves. That's why we're put on this earth."

"You're a real hedonist."

"I guess," Dylan said as the waitress set their food down and walked away without a word. Dylan had ordered several items from the menu and when the food arrived, he moved from one plate to the other until he finished. Phoenix took one bite from her eggs and realized she wasn't hungry. She pushed the plate away and sipped on her coffee.

Dylan, chewing his food, asked, "So, what do ya wanna do?"

"I've been thinking about what makes me happy."

"Yeah?"

"You make me happy."

Dylan smiled.

"I get a rush dancing."

"I know."

"But, it doesn't really mean anything, you know? There's got to be something more to life than getting homey while breaking into some idiot's house."

Dylan laughed and Phoenix allowed herself a short smile.

"So, I've been thinking about getting my G.E.D."

"You never graduated high school?"

"Long story."

"Tell me."

"Some other time, Dylan. I don't want to talk about the past right now. I want to talk about the future. If I get my G.E.D. then I can apply to Julliard. I know it's a long shot, but that's what I really want to do. I've been thinking about it every since that night at the Fox."

"Julliard?"

"A music school, in New York. Would you want to move there with me?"

"To New York? Sure."

"Maybe when we get back to St. Louis I can find a band to play with, what do you think?"

"If that's whatcha wanna do."

"I could get a lot of money for all the shit Justin and I collected over the years."

"I bet."

"I don't need all that stuff."

"No."

"I'd only really want a few things Justin gave me."

Dylan nodded.

"We could have a big yard sale, put ads in the paper."

"Sure."

Do you have anything to sell?"

"Not really, no."

"Bernard loves Justin's art collection, I'd bet he buy every piece. We could get the fuck out of St. Louis in the spring. I'd have to find out when admission is. We'd have to find a cheap apartment. Get real jobs."

The waitress came over and filled their coffees. "How we doing over here?"

"Good," Dylan answered.

"Great, thanks," said Phoenix, suddenly excited about the possibilities. She took a bite of her pancakes. "Yeah, we could do this."

"Whatever you want, baby." Dylan turned his attention again to his large breakfast.

After a few bites, Phoenix pushed her plate away and started staring out the window again.

Dylan noticed she'd become solemn again. "Justin would want this happiness for you," he said.

"I know."

"You wanna talk?"

"It's just that Justin was the first man that didn't try to manipulate me in some way. The first man who didn't treat me like a trophy piece. Or like a child," She added, thinking of Horatius Alastair. She paused for a moment then added, "But Justin was the only man I ever trusted."

Dylan set his knife down. "What am I?"

"Dylan, I love you, but I don't trust you."

He dropped his metal fork on the cheap plate, chipping it. "What? You don't trust me?"

"That's the problem, Dylan, you can't trust someone you love because when they leave you, when they hurt you, it kills a part of you. It's more painful *because* you trusted them. You trusted them not to hurt you, not to betray that trust, and they did. But if you don't trust them completely, it kinda cushions the blow, ya know? You gotta protect yourself a little. You can't be vulnerable. It's our personal security system."

"Yeah, but we break security systems."

"And steal what's inside."

Dylan, picking up his spoon to finish his soup, asked, "So you don't trust me?"

"To a certain extent, yes, I do, Dylan. But you have to understand that my trust is the last thing I give. After the companionship, the sex, the love—after all that, comes my trust."

"You have to trust first before you can fall in love."

Phoenix shook her head. "I can't. I don't want to."

"And you trusted Justin?"

"Yes."

"Do you think he betrayed you?"

"Kinda. He was leaving." Phoenix stared off. The thought of Justin deciding—choosing—to leave her, hurt her more than his actual death of which he had no control.

"I think you love Justin now more than you did when he was alive."

"Don't you dare question my love for Justin!"

"Phoenix, I know you loved him. I loved him, too, but ya gotta move on."

"Not for a while, I don't. For a while, I don't have to *move on* at all. For as long as I want, I can stagnate! As long as I feel dead from this pain, I don't have to *move* at all!"

Dylan thought about his role in Justin's death and the pain he was causing Phoenix. "I love you, you know that. I'll never do anything to hurt you again."

"What do you mean, 'again'?"

Dylan, grabbing his knife and fork, didn't know how to answer her. His eyes darted up and to the left. "I mean question your love for Justin," he began. "I mean hurt you by making you mad. I mean hurt you in any way."

––––––––––––––––

During the journey home, Dylan asked Phoenix why Justin became a thief. "With all that money, and his education, why'd he start stealing shit?"

"I never fully understood his motivation. I remember him telling me once that people rarely move out of their social class, even when committing crimes. The poor break into other poor people's houses, they kill other poor people: and the rich are the same, they rob from other rich people. It was one of his reasons for stealing guns."

"Yeah, why was that? He poured cement down the barrels."

"He told me a story about how some of the modern day martial arts weapons were actually derived from farming implements. Apparently, the Japanese warlords outlawed all weapons so they could control the peasants. Well, the peasants eventually converted these tools into some serious martial arts weapons to kick some Samurai ass. Justin's take on the whole thing was that the poor and oppressed need weapons for revolution. He said that that was the main reason for the second amendment—to keep the American feudal system in check. The rich need weapons to squash revolution and to expand their power structure. I think Justin, in his own way, was just trying to balance the scales."

"That ain't right—the rich need to protect themselves from the poor that wanna use guns to rob 'em."

"You're always going to have people robbing other people, that's not what Justin was saying. We're not talking about the guy that opens up a store in a poor neighborhood and gets robbed by one of his patrons, we're talking about the rich who are removed from the poor—those people don't have to concern themselves with being robbed. Except for the occasional, rare mugging, the wealthy are hardly ever victims of a gun-totting poor man. They're able to avoid those situations. Justin felt that weapons were misused in the hands of the elite, that's all. I think it all started with his accident."

"What accident?"

"The one where he got his scar."

"Yeah, how'd that happen?"

"He was out driving with his brother, Matthew, one night when suddenly, there was a noise—like a firecracker, only muffled, like it was under a can or something—you know?" Dylan nodded; he'd heard that sound before. "But it wasn't a firecracker, it was a gun and some guys had just shot Matthew in the head. Justin remembered laughter after the gun went off, like it was some kind of game. It was the laughter that affected Justin the most. He thought they had just blown off a firecracker, I mean these were clean-cut, all-American boys in a convertible Mercedes, right? But they were just bored rich kids who had watched too many movies. Justin told me they were probably guys he'd drank martinis with at a party once. The next thing Justin knew was they were headed straight into a ditch where they hit one of those construction barrels and flipped five times. Anyway, the drive shaft or something broke and the axel, I think, punctured the gas tank and the car caught fire. Matthew was killed and Justin broke his back and was trapped in the wreck as the car burned."

"He broke his back?"

"In two places. It took years for it to completely heal."

"Damn. Justin was made of stern stuff."

Phoenix smiled. "Yes he was." She leaned against the door and rested her head on her hands. "I'm gonna take a nap, okay?"

"Sure, honey."

Dylan let Phoenix sleep. When he pulled up to her loft, he carried her up to her bedroom. *Their bedroom.*

CHAPTER 37

When Phoenix woke up alone, she wondered why Dylan hadn't spent the night. She made some coffee, called him up, and invited him over. She then spent the good part of the morning just walking around her loft as if for the first time. Sitting on the turntable was the last album Justin had been listening to. Without looking at who it was, she set the needle down and walked away. The unmistakably voice of Leonard Cohen filled the space and she sang along to *First We Take Manhattan*.

Thinking of taking Manhattan made her think of Julliard which then made her think Of Horatius Alastair. She made a mental note to contact Julliard later to find out their admission requirements and to see if her old friend was still there. She thought about how demanding he was and vowed to herself that she would not disappoint him. The idea of seeing him again lightened her heart and as *Ain't No Cure for Love* began to play, Phoenix felt an optimism for her future she'd never experienced before. *Justin would love this*, she thought as she found herself walking into his bedroom as if to announce her decision.

She looked around his quarters and soon realized she had no reason to be there. And as Phoenix sat on Justin's bed, she slowly forgot about the music, the mood, and the thoughts of just moments ago. She felt a soothing influence wash over her that started at her forehead and cascaded through her entire body. She felt as if she were a mirage, floating just above Justin's bed. Her eyes lost focus and, for a moment, she embodied her dear friend. She was overwhelmed by his presence.

"I promise you, Justin, I will not bury the memory of you like I did with Horatius. I'll never push you to the back of my mind. You will always be a part of me." She decided she wouldn't bury her feelings to protect herself anymore. She'd allow herself to think of Justin and remember their love without any regret. She would remove the security system from her heart and throw herself into life, accepting the pain and the love. If her heart closed to protect her from pain, then it was also closed to love. She would love Dylan and trust him, just as she loved and trusted Justin. *And when—if,* she corrected her thought—*if Dylan hurts me, then I will bear that as well, but I will not be defeated!*

She rose from Justin's bed and left his room.

The thought of living alone in her apartment depressed her, and Dylan, who had shown strength and understanding throughout the ordeal of Justin's death, had earned her respect and love.

When Dylan arrived that afternoon, she asked him to move in with her.

A week later, he pulled up in his black Chevy with a few items packed in the bed. He unloaded and went back home for one more thing.

Dylan had told his father he was moving in with Phoenix in Soulard, but that he was leaving Law with him for companionship.

"I'll feed and walk him every day," Leroy assured him. "He likes those little dog biscuits, I'll go out right now and get him some."

"I'm taking Billy's bike, Dad," Dylan said almost reluctantly. "I'm not going to let it sit in there anymore gathering dust."

His father paused at the door, his hand on the doorknob.

Dylan continued, "I'm giving my bike to Phoenix, and I'm gonna ride Billy's."

Leroy Panicosky turned to him and Dylan could see the defeat in his father's eyes, the remorse, and then his father simply nodded. "It doesn't deserve to be in that garage," he said putting his car keys back in his pocket. "Go, take your things over to your new apartment. I'll put some oil and gas in his bike. The tires will need air. I'll do that, too." And his father, forgetting about Law's doggy treats, went out to the garage and pulled the cover off Billy's customized 1949 Harley Panhead.

When Dylan returned with Phoenix later that night, they went into the garage and saw Dylan and Billy's bike ready for the road. He talked about the two scooters for a few minutes and then offered his as a present to Phoenix who then opened her eyes progressively wider and wider the more the meaning and significance of his gift set in.

"What?" She asked and took a step back.

"She's yours."

"Whaddya mean?"

Dylan started to laugh. "This one is mine. And this one is yours."

"Whaddya talking about?" She practically yelled and stepped closer to the machine.

"Do you know how to ride?"

"Fuck yes I do." Phoenix recalled her lessons with her friend Wood down in Miami years ago. She approached from the left side, like one does with a horse, threw her leg over, and gently lowered herself onto the saddle. She stretched out her arms and confidently grabbed the handlebars. "One down, four up?" She asked, and Dylan, smiling proudly, nodded. She extended her left leg and flipped the kickstand back with her foot. The Harley balanced between her open thighs. She stretched out her legs then pulled them towards her, easily rolling the heavy bike back and forth. Dylan told her more about the personality of his bike, where the ignition was, how to prime the carburetors...

"I can tell you more later." Dylan handed her a helmet. "You ready?"

"Fuck yes."

They started their bikes and were about to leave the garage when Dylan noticed his father's bike was gone. In the corner was the cover folded neatly, and above that a shiny hook where his father's helmet used to rest. Dylan smiled knowing his dad rarely rode anymore, and he hoped he was out *lovin' life,* as the Panicosky's would often say while out riding.

"To lovin' life!" Dylan yelled over the rumble.

"Lovin' life!" Phoenix yelled back.

The transition from lovers living apart to living together was smooth and immediate. Dylan, accustomed to taking care of himself and his father, continued to cook for two and keep a clean house. Phoenix, spoiled by Justin who did the same, thought again of how similar the two men were. And even though she missed him terribly, she couldn't help but be happy.

Together the two moved the furniture and rearranged the posters on the wall; everything that could be moved, adjusted, changed, or altered—even the slightest bit—was. It was no longer Justin and Phoenix's apartment but Phoenix and Dylan's.

One morning Dylan woke up and Phoenix was gone. On the kitchen table he found a note that said she'd be gone for a while. He fixed himself breakfast and tried once again to call Red who used to take care of business for the Four Horsemen. He had called several times before, but Red never returned the calls. As the smoked bacon fried and crackled in the pan, Dylan called him again. When Red answered, they slipped easily into friendly conversation. Then Dylan, speaking in secret codes, told Red why he was calling: to secure a clean firearm and consult with him on a hit. They made plans to meet later that week at the Four Horsemen's private club.

Dylan hung up the phone and dropped a few eggs into the pan. They began to immediately fry in the grease left behind from the bacon. While his breakfast continued to cook, he convinced himself that under Red's tutelage, he could kill David and not get caught. When the eggs were done, he pulled the pan and absentmindedly dropped it into the sink, which accidently broke a coffee mug.

The phone rang as Dylan was eating, but he let the answering machine take it. Phoenix's voice seemed like resonance in an empty room. 'Leave a message,' was all it said. Dylan wondered why she sounded so empty, and he remembered that the day they returned, Phoenix had erased Justin's voice on the machine because it hurt too much to hear him. He told himself he'd make a new message for them after breakfast.

From the machine, came Bernard's lilting voice. "Hi, baby. How you holding up? I need to talk to you immediately—I don't care what time it is, call me, okay? And Dylan, if you're interested, I thought you and I could go out dancing. Call me."

Later that afternoon Phoenix returned home with several shopping bags full of assorted items. When she was out, she found herself going into shops at random and buying things for no reason. It wasn't until she went out of her way to go to Chin's Orient Emporium that she realized her pattern. She had gone to several of the establishments she had danced in. Inside Chin's she'd bought a pair of baggy karate pants.

When she walked into her apartment, she collapsed in a chair. "God, I forgot how exhausting shopping is."

Dylan got up from the sofa and sat at her feet. Pulling out the receipts he asked, "You mean you actually *bought* this stuff?"

"Paid cash money." Phoenix smiled and shrugged her shoulders. Dylan laughed.

He got up and kissed her on the forehead. "You want something to drink?"

"Just water."

At the tap, he called out that she had a message. "It's Bernard. It sounded important."

"I'll call him later."

"You still wanting to move to New York?"

"If I get accepted into Juilliard."

"What if you don't? Do you still wanna move?"

"Yeah, I think so."

"Where?"

"It doesn't matter, we could go anywhere. Just leave all this shit behind and go."

"Are you crazy, this stuff has to be expensive!" Dylan said, looking around the apartment.

"So what, Dylan? We can always get more stuff."

"Okay, Phoenix, sweetheart. I'll rent a U-Haul, pack all this shit up, and I'll bring all that, and you bring just your bike and a roll," Dylan said and smiled. "We'll see who stays with who."

"You'd make me sleep in a sleeping bag?" Phoenix smiled back.

"Well, if you're a good girl, you can come over and sleep on that rug there," he said pointing at a Persian rug.

"Okay, maybe we can take some of this stuff."

"It's all or nothing, babe, all or nothing."

"We can't take the espresso machine."

"No, that too."

"It's broken."

"Oh, okay, but don't break anymore things around here, and stay away from the TV."

Phoenix smiled and got up to call Bernard, hitting Dylan on the arm as she passed. Beside the phone was the mail, Phoenix picked up the small stack and rifled through it during their brief conversation where they made plans to meet later that night at a corner bar. One of the letters in her hand was the phone bill and when she opened it she noticed the name *Phoenix Sunder* on the bill. She smiled. "Attention to detail, eh Justin?"

The next letter she opened was the application to Juilliard; she smiled wider when she saw the requirements to get in. After she received her G.E.D., *the rest of the process would be a breeze*, she thought. She felt confident that she'd be able to pass the hardest step, that of the live audition, with the help of a good teacher—*If I can find one in St. Louis.* She also discovered Horatius Alastair was still at Julliard and decided, when she was ready, she'd send him a tape and ask him for a letter of recommendation. The thought of playing for him again thrilled her and she decided to practice more Coltrane, one of his favorites.

CHAPTER 38

Phoenix ordered a beer, sat at a booth, and waited for Bernard. A feeling of ennui overcame her. *Why did he want to meet here?* She was apprehensive, uneasy. Something she couldn't explain or identify made her irritable. She looked around the bar and so no familiar faces. *Fuck this.* She finished her beer and was about to leave when Bernard walked in. When he sat down, Phoenix could see the somber mood he was in. Suddenly Phoenix didn't want to hear anything Bernard had to say.

"You okay?" Bernard asked lighting a cigarette. "Yes."

"Dylan here?"

"Do you see him?"

"I don't know how to start this."

"If it's bad, I don't want to hear it."

"It's bad."

"Then I don't want to hear it." She slid out of the booth and went to the bar to order a shot."

"Phoenix," Bernard called out from the booth.

"What!" she demanded.

"Come here."

Phoenix walked over to Bernard and sat down.

"Remember when I came back from Mexico," Bernard began, "and found out Justin was killed and he was found on the north side?"

"Yes."

"You know he didn't get killed there, right? He wouldn't be walking alone on the north side, right?"

"Probably not"

"Definitely not."

"What then?"

"You know what happened," Bernard said.

Fuck.

"It was David."

Phoenix's air left her lungs. *Fuck.* She sat there silent, stirring her drink. "I was afraid of that," she said looking into her glass. "How do you know?"

"I was with him last night. I've been trying to avoid him every since I heard you fucking idiots broke into his condo, but he came over to my house, and I couldn't do nothin' about it. I knew something was seriously wrong, that this was no social call, but I tried to be cool. After a few minutes of talking about Mexico, Kevin gets up and goes to the door and just stands there. And I'm thinking, 'oh my God, I'm gonna die!' and David looks into my eyes the way he does—he's a fucking mind reader, I'm telling you—and he's staring at me and asking me about Justin, and I knew right then he killed him. I know how he is. He asked my why I lied to Kevin about being with Justin down at the lake the weekend he was ripped off—no, he didn't say ripped off, he said, *danced.* Phoenix, he said danced."

She closed her eyes and dropped her head.

"Anyway, I told him I didn't lie to Kevin, we really were down at the lake. Then I lied to him about how Justin couldn't have done it, why he couldn't have done it. I don't know what I said or how I said it, but he bought it. So, then he started asking about you."

Phoenix shook her head and lit a cigarette.

"I convinced him that since you met Dylan, you and Justin didn't hang out at all anymore—which is true," he added accusingly.

"So, are me and Dylan safe?"

"I think so."

"Thank you, Bernard."

"Don't thank me yet. There's more."

"What?"

"The *dance* thing. It took me a while before it all made sense. Dance. Who says *dance*, Phoenix? Me, you and Dylan," he said, not waiting for an answer. "That's it—me, you and *Dylan*. If David hadn't said, 'dance,' I never would've figured it out."

"Figured what out?" Phoenix asked softly. She, too, realized the significance of David quoting their private slang.

"The only person that knew, and could have told David, and used 'dance' when he told him, is Dylan."

"Don't be stupid, Bernard!"

"Did you tell Dylan that I knew about it?"

"Don't be a jealous ass, Barnard!"

"Did anybody else know about this, Phoenix?"

"I don't know, maybe."

"Please, nobody else knew about this, Phoenix, if they did, they would've given everybody's names—yours, Dylan's, *as well as* Justin's. They wouldn't have singled out just him. It would have been Justin and you, maybe Dylan, but definitely you."

"No."

"Dylan—your fucking boyfriend—got Justin killed! I don't know why, and I don't care. I know what I know. I know that David killed Justin and it was that son of a bitch Dylan who pointed him in Justin's direction."

"Not Dylan," Phoenix said trying to convince herself. "He loved him."

"No, he didn't."

Phoenix recalled the night Justin announced he was leaving. She remembered feeling odd that entire day, like she was hungry or tired, but whenever she tried to eat or sleep, she couldn't. When she cornered Justin at home and he told her of his plans to leave, it was then she realized what her body had confused for lack of food or sleep was in fact her soul's intuition of her impending loss.

CHAPTER 39

In Forest Park Phoenix and Dylan lay on a hill overlooking a large manmade lake. It was the dead of winter and the large park in the middle of the city was cold and barren. The ground, hard and frozen. Looming behind the lone couple in the deserted park stood a pavilion of white stone and red tile. Above, the stars offered little inspiration for Phoenix. The Little Dipper hanging from the North Star and parts of what Phoenix thought was Orion were all she could see past the dark clouds. Suspended between the branches of a large, naked maple tree, the moon, partially covered by clouds, looked down upon Phoenix and Dylan.

"Justin and I used to come here all the time when we ate mushrooms," Phoenix said. "One night he became so aware of his being, he swore he could count the rings on a living tree just by touching its bark." She laughed. "Said it was driving him crazy."

After a moment Dylan said, "I miss him, more than I thought I would. I wish he was still alive. If I'd been with him, I could've stopped it. I know I could've. I could've helped him defend himself."

Dylan spoke with such sincerity, almost blaming himself for not being at Justin's side, that Phoenix believed him—believed *in* him—and she started to doubt Bernard's accusations.

"Bernard was talking about that the other night," she said.

"He was?" *Why?*

"He was wondering what would make someone kill another person."

"Greed, stupidity, jealousy... millions of reasons and in the end no reason at all. Life is too important for anybody else to take it away.

You can't rob somebody of their life; that ain't right. People just can't go around killing people just because they're different..." Dylan said, thinking of his brother. Billy wearing his colors was the only tag the other club needed to murder him.

Phoenix noticed Dylan's change and saw he was upset. "Bernard's a fool," she said, barely audible, but Dylan heard her.

"Where did that come from?" he asked, trying to laugh. But Phoenix was silent. "What was Bernard saying?"

"Nothing!"

"Was he talking about me?"

Phoenix didn't answer.

"What was he saying?" Dylan demanded.

"He was just talking about who killed Justin."

"Does he think it was *me*?" Dylan asked, sitting up. When Phoenix offered no response, He stood up. "Jesus Christ—he does!"

"No," is all Phoenix could say.

"No? What do you mean—no? Why else would he mention me?"

"Dylan..." Phoenix said, getting up and moving toward him.

"I didn't kill Justin—I don't know what that faggot is talking about!"

Phoenix reached out for him. "He didn't say..."

"But I'll tell you one thing," Dylan interrupted, moving away from Phoenix's arms. "I'm gonna kill the motherfucker that did. I can tell you that! I'm gonna blow his fucking head off!"

Phoenix stood still while Dylan paced around her, gesturing in the night.

"I don't wanna kill anybody, believe me I don't. This isn't an easy thing to do, but people have to be held responsible. Bad things happen to everybody, but you have to take responsibility for your own actions. You can't make excuses. I've made mistakes, you have, we all have; but I'm gonna correct mine. David kills Justin, and he don't think he has to pay? He pays. Somebody makes him fucking pay, no excuses."

Phoenix turned her head to Dylan.

"And I don't care what you think," Dylan continued. "You may hate this violence crap; you may think it's primitive. You may hate me, but that's the way it is. It's that simple. David's dead. I'm gonna see to it. Would Bernard avenge Justin?"

"Dylan, honey, don't mess with David. He's crazy..."

Dylan stood there, shaking, nervous, and reached out to hold Phoenix to calm his nature. But she looked at him strangely and took a half step backward. "What?" he asked.

Phoenix's eyes set wide upon Dylan and saw him clearer now than she had all night. The clouds that hindered the night's light had moved away, for just a second, and then it was dark again. She remembered Bernard telling her that they were the only ones who knew David killed Justin, the only ones: Bernard and her. *How did Dylan know?*

"What did you say about David?"

"Don't try to talk me out of it, Phoenix. I take care of me and mine."

"But how do you know it was David?"

For Dylan, for a moment, everything stopped. His eyes widened indiscernibly in the night as he realized that he just incriminated himself. "I heard it tonight." Dylan's eyes darted up and to the left. "I was gonna tell you that ... didn't I tell you that?"

"You heard tonight? Just like that? You just happen to overhear somebody announce that David killed Justin?"

"No, it wasn't just like that Phoenix—I—you know—I've got connections—fuck! The Four Horsemen know how to gather Intel. Damn, I'm not some idiot, ya know?"

Phoenix sat down. The park was dark again. The wind died. The noises from the city ceased; the only scent Phoenix knew was the fragrance of winter, that somehow smelled of rust—her body, heavy, pushed to the ground, numb. "Oh, Dylan."

"But I'm gonna get him," he said, "I got a plan."

Dylan Panicosky paced on the frozen ground and Phoenix heard it cracking.

CHAPTER 40

That night, Phoenix made plans to spend the night with Stephanie.

"What's wrong?" Dylan asked before she left their loft.

"Nothing. I just want to visit an old friend, Dylan. Is it okay if I visit an old friend? Someone I've known longer than you?"

"Yeah, sure."

Phoenix grabbed her saxophone, the keys to Justin's Nova, and left.

At Stephanie's apartment in the Shaw neighborhood, Phoenix sat on a worn loveseat under a single floor lamp in the corner, her feet resting on an old wooden coffee table. She stared at the black screen of a small TV sitting on cinder blocks. The stereo was turned to a blues station and the music playing was Coltrane. She could hear cars driving pass on the quiet street outside.

Phoenix rose from the loveseat and paced the wooden floor. Stephanie's apartment was large but empty. She walked down the hallway to the kitchen and saw an art-deco table with four plastic chairs; she entered Stephanie's bedroom that had a large bed, one simple dresser, and a floor length mirror. She thought about all the beautiful things she and Justin had in their apartment that now seemed so cold and hard and uninviting. She wanted to go back to her loft for the marble and glass phoenix and then leave a match behind for the rest.

Phoenix approached Stephanie's third floor window that overlooked Shaw's Botanical Garden and looked out into the black and white night. She knew behind the line of trees before her rested the Japanese garden. She and Justin had walked through it soon after they'd met, and Justin told her about the Tea House on the tiny island in the large pond.

"It has a small door," Justin had told her as they'd crossed the arched bridge. "Low, near the ground, so samurai, merchant and peasant had to crawl in, on hands and knees, in the same humble fashion. Once inside, they were same. Nobody was better than the other."

Phoenix was inside the peaceful, quiet garden and she could see Justin leaning against the wooden bridge. She could feel the wind tossing her hair aside.

When she stepped away from the window, leaving the garden, she realized she'd been there, in her mind, for over an hour. She picked up the phone to call home, wanting to talk to Justin. When the phone rang once, she remembered he wasn't there anymore and hung up. She then found George Sitting Wolf's phone number in her bag and decided to call him. George listened as Phoenix talked about Justin, Dylan, Bernard, David, and Horatius. Her confessions, her doubts, her honesty, all affected Sitting Wolf. Phoenix purged herself behind the phone and cried for the first time in her life with abandonment and Sitting Wolf listened.

"I'm sorry, George."

"Please, Phoenix, call me Sitting Wolf. And you've done nothing to apologize for."

"I shouldn't have called. I just needed somebody. Justin respected you; he turned to you for help. I guess I wanted to do the same. I didn't know who else to call."

"You've lived a hard life, daughter. When we are forced to face our demons, few have the strength you've shown; and when we are forced to face the demons of others, even fewer can move among them unscathed. You have done well, Phoenix, your name is no mistake. Justin was about to leave his life behind to find his history. I think you are about to leave your life behind to find your future."

"Can you help me?"

"I cannot. You know what to do, I hear you speak. Just like Justin knew what to do. Do not wait until it is too late to do the right thing, like Justin Falling Leaf.

"Was that his Indian name?

"It would have been, if he wanted it. His grandfather called him that at his birth. If you ever need to get away, to clear your mind, you can always come here."

She chuckled slightly. "I may take you up on that sooner than you think."

The two finished talking as snow began to fall. Phoenix grabbed her saxophone, turned off all the lights, and sat by the window. She absentmindedly caressed her chest, her fingers drawn over the serpent-shaped scar that rested there. She sucked on the reed of her saxophone and watched the falling snow. In her mind, she heard a melody, soft and sensual, with an adagio tempo. Phoenix listened to the tune, thinking it sounded familiar, trying to place it, but couldn't. She began fingering the keys, and breathing into on her instrument. Soon Stephanie's apartment was filled with Phoenix's voice as she gave birth to her first composition: Falling Leaf.

CHAPTER 41

Dylan woke up the next morning alone. He called Stephanie's but Phoenix was out. He then called Bernard and agreed to go dancing with him. Forgetting about the threat of David, he plotted his vengeance against Bernard. They made plans to dance the next night.

"Why not tonight?" Dylan asked.

"David told me the people who live there will be gone Friday night"

"David told you about this?"

"Yeah."

David had told Bernard about the house after their last conversation. At the time, Bernard felt obligated to accept David's mission. After Bernard had put all the players in Justin's death together, he willingly went into what he knew was a trap set by David. But Bernard had other plans.

"You want to do this or not?" Bernard asked Dylan.

Dylan felt uncomfortable going to a dance arranged by David. "I didn't know you and him were friends."

"He gives me leads every now and then." Bernard lied. "Usually I'd give it to Phoenix and Justin, but that's all changed now."

"Did David know Justin and Phoenix helped you out?"

"Hell no," he said, then added: "And I didn't tell Phoenix about this one 'cause I thought you'd might like to be the bread winner, you know, fill Justin's shoes. For her."

"Yeah, Bernard, for Phoenix. Okay, sure." Dylan hung up the phone then went into Justin's room where he went through Justin's gun collection to find the only gun without cement down its barrel, the

9mm Smith and Wesson. "Yes indeed. Yeah, Bernard, okay. I'll dance on your grave! Anything else you want to tell Phoenix? No? Good!"

Dylan tried again to call Phoenix, but no one answered the phone. He spent the rest of the day getting drunk, enjoying the luxury around him

In the morning, he called Phoenix again and was told by Stephanie that she was out. "Have you been telling her I'm calling?"

"Dylan, I haven't seen her. She's depressed and needs to be alone and I don't know where she is. When she's ready I'm sure you'll be the first one she calls, okay?"

"Sure."

"Be patient, Dylan."

"Yeah, sure." *Fucking Bernard*. He spent the day drinking the vodka Justin had chilled in the freezer. When night arrived, Dylan left the apartment and got on his bike. The snow from the previous night had melted off the roads, but the weather was still cold, and Dylan wanted the wind to hit him full in the face, chill him through his leather jacket and leather pants, turn his gloveless hands white. He rode his bike recklessly in and out of traffic.

When he pulled up in front of Bernard's house, he turned off his bike and its lone eye closed. He sat there watching the last glow of the sun sink below the horizon. It was a beautiful sunset, he thought, full of blood colors.

When he walked into Bernard's apartment, he took off his jacket and hung it on a pink hall tree with six bent rubber penises pointing up. He sat down on the white upholstered sofa with black stick figures drawn all over it and drank the tequila shot Bernard gave him.

"You want to play a game of cards before we leave?" Bernard asked lighting a joint.

"Sure," Dylan said, reluctantly taking a hit from the joint that was just in Bernard's mouth.

The two smoked, drank, and played cards for an hour, Bernard winning as often as he lost, but Dylan, betting more aggressively, seemed to win the bigger hands that piled up in front of him. Bernard upped the ante a dollar from his neatly stacked bank and looked up at the cuckoo clock on the wall; his brother-in-law would be expecting them in less than an hour, waiting with the other cops for Dylan to break into the house. Bernard, who wanted to avenge Justin but couldn't murder Dylan in cold blood, had tipped off his brother-in-law, a St. Louis police officer, that the man responsible for the string of robberies over the past couple of years was Dylan Panicosky. Bernard told his brother-in-law the location of Dylan's next mark. If everything went as expected, David would be in there too.

Dylan, noticing Bernard looking at the clock, asked when they were leaving.

"Oh, honey, calm down. Keep your shorts on. You're so impetuous!"

"I think you're pretty wasted tonight. Be careful."

"Are you kidding? I can piss and walk on water."

Dylan looked at his cards and threw them down. "Fuck this shit. Let's go!"

Bernard agreed, and the two men walked out the door, smiling at each other.

Outside the window of the chosen house, Bernard watched Dylan perform one of Phoenix's favorite breaking and entering tricks. He covered the window with duct tape, tapped the window with his flashlight, then peeled away the broken glass.

Inside, Dylan felt the hard weight of his gun, and not knowing when or where to kill Bernard, he waited; and while he waited, he grabbed a VCR. Dylan went from room to room and deliberately picked out the items he wanted. When he walked in the bedroom, he saw a man sitting on the bed and another man standing in the corner. David and Kevin, who were expecting Bernard, weren't shocked when they saw a man walk through the door, but Dylan, who had no idea they were there, instantly froze: "Who the fuck are you!"

Kevin pointed his gun at the silhouette in the doorway. David, realizing it wasn't Bernard, asked, "No, who the fuck are you?"

Downstairs, Bernard heard the voices and knew his plan had worked. He crawled through the window and hid behind a large oak.

In the bedroom, Dylan finally recognized who he was talking to and revised his plan to include killing David and Kevin. He smiled at his luck. "Well, if it ain't David. How ya doin' there Davo?" Dylan thought about his gun tucked in his pants. He set the bag down full of stolen goods.

David looked closer at Dylan. "What the hell are you doing here?"

"I came with Bernard."

Kevin lowered his gun. "Where is he?"

"Downstairs."

As Kevin left the bedroom, Dylan pulled his gun out and hid it behind his back.

"What are you doing here?" Dylan asked.

"We're waiting for Bernard."

Dylan laughed. "You're gonna kill him, that's why you sent him here."

David smiled.

"That's funny," Dylan said, "because I was gonna kill him tonight. But you want to know something that's even funnier? I'm also gonna kill you." Dylan pointed his gun at David.

David dropped his smile. "And why do you want to kill me?"

"Because you killed Justin."

"What?" David laughed. "You told me about him. You killed Justin, my friend."

Just then Kevin came running in, "Bernard's gone—" Dylan turned to Kevin and shot him in the face.

Outside, Bernard watched three squad cars pull up, silently, forebodingly, and watched them get out of their cars. When the shot rang out the police saturated the house with their strong white lights.

Inside the house, Dylan had his gun pointed at David's chest. A police siren squawked twice. Dylan crossed to the window and looked out to see the cops positioning themselves. "Fuck you," he said to them, "And fuck you," he said to David and shot him twice in the chest before running downstairs.

Outside a police officer was on the bullhorn. Snow began to fall again, Bernard looked through the soft curtain of snow and watched his brother-in-law and the other officers wait for Dylan to emerge.

Suddenly Dylan bolted out the back door and the night was lit from the fire of Dylan's gun and the return fire from the officers'. Bernard watched the lightning that pierced the night; he heard the shouts from Dylan and the officers as they shot. He watched Dylan running across the yard like a performer in a macabre dance. As the police lights reflected off the white vale of snow, Bernard could clearly see Dylan Panicosky fall.

CHAPTER 42

When Phoenix heard the news from Bernard, she was surprisingly calm. Bernard thought she had a look of surrender, of defeat, but Phoenix had simply allowed the past month to wash over her and she accepted everything with heavy but strong resolve. "It was pretty clever of you, the way you set the whole thing up," she offered, then smiled at Bernard.

"I guess there's a new Al Capone in this town—an Alice Capone! Well, anyway, here's the money for Justin's art collection."

"Baby, for all you've done, I really wish you'd just take it."

"No, you've priced everything really well; it's worth it, I want it, you need the money. It's done. But I will take a few plants though."

"You got it, sweetie."

Bernard gave her a kiss and left. "I'll see ya later."

Stephanie showed up with Carl and the two meticulously went through Justin and Phoenix's extensive music collection, quickly filling two plastic milk crates. Ginny, carrying a box of several kitchen appliances walked up to Phoenix and handed her $200.

After everybody left, Phoenix took a long bath and ruminated on her impending visit to Sitting Wolf. She lit a joint and blew smoke across the water, skimming the top, creating a mist above her body. In the shallow tub, she became lost in deep thoughts. The phone rang in the other room but Phoenix was apathetic about its heralding.

"Hi, baby, where are you?" Dylan asked the machine. "Did you get my messages? I'll be out of the hospital next Thursday, but the pigs here are taking me straight downtown. They're not letting me post bail.

These sons-of-bitches think I'm responsible for a goddamn crime-wave! They said I killed a cop. I need you to pay for a good lawyer to stand up for me. I'll pay you back, baby. I've got to get out of here. You know how this kills me. Thanks, honey, I love you. I'm waiting for you."

The next day Dylan called again. "Phoenix, I'm not taking the rap for all the shit Justin did. You'd better get down here and talk to me. I told these pigs that Justin broke into all those places, but they seem to think he had an accomplice. They think it was me, but we know it wasn't—don't we. You help me and I'll help you. Now, I know you didn't have anything to do with all these break-ins, but the police have been asking me questions about you. I don't know how they got your name."

Over the next several days, friends and strangers came by and slowly bought everything in her loft that was for sale. She had placed ads for the expensive furniture, lights, and rugs—at a quarter of their original price—and had gotten an immediate and overwhelming response. Nobody haggled with her. Danny-boy bought the entertainment center and all that it housed. John Bowman bought her and Dylan's motorcycles. Jeanette bought all of Justin's clothes and several items of Phoenix's.

Dylan left three more messages, each one emphasizing his love and devotion, followed by increasing threats, countered with promises of fidelity. Leroy even called her once and his supplication almost caused Phoenix to call him back.

One cold morning, soon after the New Year, Phoenix left St. Louis to convalesce with Sitting Wolf at his ranch in Oregon. There, inspired by the beauty she'd never observed before, she cultivated her talents and prepared for her audition into Julliard.

Phoenix Sunder landed in Lambert International Airport in St. Louis, Missouri and was immediately wrapped in its suffocating heat. She'd been gone for 20 years and very little had changed. She rented a car and drove through her old stomping grounds, and felt no connection to the city that was so instrumental in her transformation. She had slowly lost touch with her St. Louis friends and was secretly hoping none of them would try to contact her while she was in town for her performance at The Fox. The blighted areas she knew during her scarred stay had been replaced with renewal and renovation but she still felt no life there. As she wandered, she recalled the familiar darkness she'd cloaked herself in. She thought of the deceit and despair that had threatened to engulf her, and she thought of Dylan.

It's the bad boy who gets the young girl's heart.

Phoenix carried Justin with her always, but St. Louis reminded her of Dylan Panicosky.

The End

ABOUT THE AUTHOR

Mark Pannebecker graduated from Webster University where he majored in film/video production and minored in lit/lang with an acute interest in philosophy. He's produced and directed several films including an award-winning short he wrote. However, the process of writing seduced him away from the camera and he's spent his post graduation years traveling and writing fiction. He's recently published a collection of poetry titled Motorcycle Boy Lives and a collection of short stories titled Godsfood. Fraternity of Fractures is his first novel to be published.

You can visit him at www.markpannebecker.com

Printed in the United States
By Bookmasters